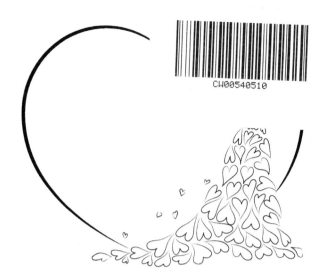

MINE TO LOVE

Presley

After my sisters' disastrous weddings, I'm never going to get married.
I'll just stay single forever.
It doesn't matter that I'm in love with my brother's best friend.
Or that Bennett and I shouldn't even be friends with benefits.
Until the positive sign tells me I'm pregnant.

Bennett

I fell in love with Presley when she was eighteen and asked me for a favor.
She didn't want to go to college as a virgin.
I said no, but she kissed me, and I was lost in her.
Years later, I'll take her with any rules she gives me.
She thinks this is just a fling, but she's wrong.
Because she's always been mine to love.

BOOKS BY NATASHA MADISON

Southern Wedding Series
Mine To Kiss

Mine To Have

Mine To Cherish

Mine to Love

The Only One Series
Only One Kiss

Only One Chance

Only One Night

Only One Touch

Only One Regret

Only One Mistake

Only One Love

Only One Forever

Southern Series
Southern Chance

Southern Comfort

Southern Storm

Southern Sunrise

Southern Heart

Southern Heat

Southern Secrets

Southern Sunshine

This Is
This is Crazy

This Is Wild

This Is Love

This Is Forever

Hollywood Royalty
Hollywood Playboy

Hollywood Princess

Hollywood Prince

Something So Series
Something Series

Something So Right

Something So Perfect

Something So Irresistible

Something So Unscripted

Something So BOX SET

Tempt Series
Tempt The Boss

Tempt The Playboy

Tempt The Ex

Tempt The Hookup

Heaven & Hell Series

Hell And Back

Pieces Of Heaven

Love Series
Perfect Love Story

Unexpected Love Story

Broken Love Story

Faux Pas

Mixed Up Love

Until Brandon

SOUTHERN WEDDING SERIES TREE

Mine To Have
Harlow Barnes & Travis Baker

Mine To Hold
Shelby Baker & Ace

Mine To Cherish
Clarabella & Luke

Mine To Love
Presley & Bennett

Southern Family tree
Billy and Charlotte
(Mother and father to Kallie and Casey)

Southern Chance
Kallie & Jacob McIntyre
Ethan McIntyre (Savannah Son)
Amelia
Travis

Southern Comfort
Olivia & Casey Barnes
Quinn (Southern Heat)
Reed (Southern Sunshine)
Harlow (Mine to Have)

Southern Storm
Savannah & Beau Huntington
Ethan McIntyre (Jacob's son)
Chelsea (Southern Heart)
Toby
Keith

Southern Sunrise
Emily & Ethan McIntyre
Gabriel
Aubrey

Southern Heart
Chelsea Huntington & Mayson Carey
Tucker

Southern Heat
Willow & Quinn Barnes

Southern Secrets
Amelia McIntyre & Asher

Southern Sunshine
Hazel & Reed Barnes
Sophia

Cover Design: Jay Aheer
Photo by Regina Wamba

Editing done by Jenny Sims Editing4Indies

Proofing Julie Deaton by Deaton Author Services

Proofing by Judy's proofreading

Formatting by Christina Parker Smith

mine to LOVE

Southern Wedding Series

NATASHA MADISON

*P*rologue

*D*earest Love,

For the first time, no one is getting married.

I so hoped Presley would find the one and bite the bullet, but no can do.

Or at least that is what I thought.

But...

A little plus sign has changed it all. Now, it's getting a little sticky. Especially since the dad-to-be is ready to get down on bended knee.

He's going to need a miracle to get her to walk down that aisle!

Time will tell!

XOXO

NM

One

Presley

I tap the steering wheel with my perfectly manicured nail as I sing along to the song blasting from the radio when I pull up to the office. I park my car next to my sisters', then grab my iced latte and my new Yves St. Laurent bag. Putting my purse under my arm, I shut the door and take a look around, seeing the flowers starting to bloom on the trees. When my sisters and I decided to go into business together, we got the idea from our mom and aunt, who ran a small wedding planning business. But the three of us didn't just want to plan weddings. No, we wanted to be the best event planners in the business, and with that came the idea to build our own event space. We bought a huge piece of land and slowly built it up.

Our main offices were in a nice little bungalow we built with three offices upstairs where the bedrooms would be, and the downstairs was a little setup of things we have done along with pictures from all our events. I look off toward the right and see the food truck as well. The main thing that took the longest to build was the actual event building.

It looks like a barn from the outside, but once you get inside, you'll find rustic wooden floors and exposed wooden beams that can be dressed up. It can fit up to five hundred and fifty people. Right behind the barn is a kitchen where the caterers can set up.

I smile, turning and making my way up the stairs. The sound of my heels on the concrete steps echoes in the quietness of the morning.

I grab the door handle, pull it open, and step in. The cold air hits me right away. Stepping in, I see Clarabella and Shelby standing in the waiting area. I take a big inhale. "You know what that smells like?" I smile, looking at both of them. They stand in front of me. Clarabella in blue pants and a white top. Shelby in white jeans and a silk pink tank top.

"Like you've had sex?" Clarabella says, looking at me. I glare at her, but she can't see since my black sunglasses hide my eyes. She brings her cup of coffee to her lips, trying to hide the smile behind it, but her blue eyes squint.

"No, asshole," I say, "it smells like wedding season."

"It smelled like cow shit when I drove up today," Shelby complains, her face grimaced. "But I guess I should see the glass half full."

"Oh, come on," I urge, lifting my glasses on top of my head. "It's sunny and beautiful outside." I point at the open shade as the sun shines into the office. "It's going to be a great day."

"I don't like this, Presley." Clarabella points at me. "Ever since you got into the Zen shit, it's like I don't even know who you are."

"It's not about being Zen. It's about looking for the good in the day," I say, walking down the hallway toward my office. I pass Shelby's and Clarabella's offices. Mine is all the way in the back with all the windows.

"I blame you," Clarabella accuses. I look over my shoulder as she glares at Shelby, who just stands there with her mouth open.

"Why me?" she shrieks and points at her chest.

"You got her that *eat, pray, love* bullshit diary," Clarabella says, shaking her head and turning to follow me into my office. "Tell me five things that made you smile today," she mimics one of the questions in the book. "Take a minute to tell us what went wrong but, in the end, didn't change the outcome." I chuckle at her as I walk around my desk, putting my iced coffee down on the coaster before walking over to the blinds and opening them to let the sun shine in.

"I got you the same one," Shelby points out. "And you stayed normal." They both walk into my office, going over to sit on the white loveseat I have against the wall that faces my desk.

"It has to be the sex, then." Clarabella looks at me, and

I pinch my eyebrows together, admitting nothing. Trying to portray the cool collectiveness that I'm attempting to channel.

"I have no idea what you're talking about," I lie through my teeth. "I got up at five o'clock today." I sit down in the office chair. "After I worked out, I had my coffee and counted my blessings."

"She's broken," Shelby declares, looking at Clarabella while I laugh. "I fucking broke her."

"I'm not broken," I say, shaking my head, and I wince when I cross my legs. Rolling my lips because it has nothing to do with the workout. Did I wake up at five o'clock today? I did. Did I do it to work out? Some would call sex the best workout you can get. Did I want to admit this to my sisters? Absolutely not. "Maybe I'm maturing." I grab the iced coffee and bring the cup to my lips. "I mean, I'm going to be thirty in a couple of months, after all."

"Oh, here she goes." Shelby rolls her eyes.

"Don't here we go." I hold up my hand. "We have so much to be thankful for."

"I'm leaving." Clarabella stands. "If she's going to go all eat, pray, love, I'm going to throw up that amazing breakfast my husband made me this morning." She mentions her husband, Luke, who is one of the best cooks out there.

"Okay, fine," I huff. "I'm just going to say it'll be nice to go into the wedding season with neither of you getting married." I smile. "It's less stress to not have to worry if the wedding is actually going to take place." I point at both of them. "Between Travis and his almost first wedding. To you becoming a legend for walking down the aisle and then fucking off." I point at Shelby. "And to you for being a runaway bride." I point at Clarabella.

"I wasn't a runaway bride," she huffs. "I left." I tilt my head to the side. "Quickly." I raise my eyebrows at her. "In a truck."

"Literally left the scene of the crime." Shelby gets up now, laughing. "Leaving the murder weapon behind."

"Well, she did leave with a different murder weapon." I chuckle at my pun and take another sip of the iced coffee. "He murdered her vagina with it."

"That he did," Clarabella admits. "He still does it." She smiles wide. "Now, are we going to discuss sex lives because if that's the case." She turns the tables on me and tilts her head. "How about you go first?"

"Don't you two have work to do?" I glare at her, then turn my glare to Shelby. "Isn't there a phone that you need to go and have sex on?"

Shelby rolls her eyes at me. "When your man starts traveling—"

"I don't have a man," I cut her off quickly.

"Okay, fine. If your 'friend'"—she makes air quotes— "'travels, you tell me you won't have phone sex."

"You can go without sex for a week. You won't die." I lean back in the chair.

"Not when you have good sex," Clarabella states. "It's like a drug."

I roll my eyes. "You can both go now," I say, ignoring the way they snicker at each other as they walk out of the room. I turn on my computer and work on returning emails and phone calls. The three of us all deal with different aspects of the planning. Clarabella takes care of the food and drinks. Shelby does the decorations, and I meet with the couples and we go over scheduling of events. I look over my calendar and set two alarms on my phone for when I have to be ready for meetings.

I meet with two brides who I make a note to call back tomorrow for confirmation, and when I finally look outside, I see the sun is starting to go down, and the office is eerily quiet. The phone rings in my hand, and I look down and see his name. Bennett is calling. My stomach gets tight, and my heart speeds up, but I push it all down and away. I think about not answering, but by the second ring, my finger is swiping the screen. "Presley Baker." I close my eyes when I hear his chuckle.

"Hey, gorgeous." His voice comes out smooth, and right away, I'm back to being sixteen years old. It was then that I fell in love with him. He was and still is my brother Travis's best friend and, to this day, the only man I've ever fucking been with. "Where are you?"

"Work," I say, walking back to my office. "Where are you?"

"Just got out of a meeting." I hear him huff out, and then a car door slams, and I know he's in his car. "What are we doing for dinner?" he asks me, and I roll my eyes. "You can stop rolling your eyes, gorgeous."

"One, I've told you to stop calling me that." *But you love it*, my head screams out to me. "And two, I didn't roll my eyes." I hear him chuckle, and the butterflies start in my stomach. "And three, I'm busy."

"Really?" he says as I hear the call switch from his phone to his Bluetooth. "That's too bad because I was going to grab a couple of those burgers from the place you like."

"Smooth." I look at the clock. "When will you be home?"

"About forty-five minutes," he says, and I think about an excuse. I should just go home and soak in a tub.

What I should not do, is go to him. "Fine, I'll meet you at your place." I don't even bother saying goodbye. I just disconnect on him. I ignore the laughing in my head while I close up my things, and forty-five minutes later, I pull up to his house at the same time as he does. I'm about to open my door when I turn and see him there opening the door for me. "Annoying," I mumble when he holds his hand out to me, and I grab it. The hammering in my chest calms as soon as I step out and come face-to-face with him.

His black hair pushed back to the side, his five o'clock shadow already showing. His musky smell fills my nose as he takes a step in. "Hi, gorgeous," he says, wrapping one arm around my waist and then bending to kiss my lips. "I missed you."

Two

Bennett

I wait for her to walk out of the bedroom before I open my eyes, blinking a couple of times to get used to the darkness. The sound of her creeping around the bedroom always wakes me up. I flip the covers off me and get out, grabbing my boxers that were thrown on the floor last night when we got upstairs. It started on the couch, and then by the time we got upstairs, we were both frantic with need. There was a trail of clothing all the way to the bedroom. I smile to myself, knowing she's going to be searching for her panties that I tucked into the couch when I pulled her on me to straddle my lap.

Walking out of the bedroom, I try my best not to make any noise. The sun is slowly coming up, but it's still dark out, yet I can make out her face with the soft light coming from the kitchen. Every time I see her, I'm always taken aback by how gorgeous she is. She tucks a piece of her hair behind her ear as she moves from the stairs to the living room, picking up the discarded clothes as she makes her way around the house.

I see her looking for her panties and have to roll my lips before I make a noise. She finally gives up, grabbing one of her shoes and then walking a couple more steps until she finds the other one. She doesn't put them on for fear that she will make a noise. I take a couple of steps down until I'm in the middle of the staircase. I see her grabbing her purse that she left on the table in the hallway. She holds her shoes and purse close to her chest as she tiptoes to the front door. Her black hair sways side to side as she makes her way to the door. I shake my head. She's snuck out of my house every time she's stayed here. I wait for her hand to unlock the door before I speak. "See you tonight." Her hand stops on the handle, and her body goes tense. It's the first time I've gotten out of bed and confronted her on her way out. "Do you want to stay and have some coffee?" I roll my lips when she shakes her head and opens the door. "Have a good day, gorgeous." She doesn't turn back to look at me. Instead, she walks out and slams the door behind her, making me burst out laughing. "Presley, Presley, Presley," I say to myself as I walk down the rest of the steps toward the front door.

Pulling it open, I lean against the doorjamb and watch her walk to her car. The whole time, my eyes are on her perfect ass. Folding my arms over my chest, I look around the neighborhood, finding not one single house has lights on. The only sounds are the birds chirping. She looks over at me when she opens her car door, and I see the smile she is trying to hide by rolling her eyes as she gets into her car. When she looks over at me, it's with a glare as I smile and wave at her, no doubt pissing her off even more. She takes off with her head shaking, and I wait until I can't see her before I walk back into the house and close the door behind me. "I'm so fucked," I say out loud as I walk over to the kitchen and see that it's just a little bit after five in the morning. Turning on the television to the news, I make my coffee, wishing she'd stayed. My chest gets tight when I think about it, and I ignore it just like I always do.

Getting involved with Presley was the best thing that I've ever done, hands down, and a decision I will never, ever regret. Was it a smart move? Probably not. Did I want to go back and change how it happened? Fuck no. It was our history, and it was always going to be how we became. Was I tired of her sneaking out all the time and not staying? One hundred and fifty million percent yes.

Twelve years ago, I was at the bar a town over when I spotted her coming in. She had just turned eighteen a couple of months before, so I knew she had a fake ID to even get into this place. I watched her laugh with a couple of friends before she felt me staring, and when she did, she looked up at the ceiling. She also mouthed, "Motherfucker," before she came over to me. My cock literally rose to the occasion, and I internally yelled at it, telling him that she was off-limits. I knew the look she was giving me was trouble. I just didn't know how much. I leaned into the bar and ignored the way my body was reacting to her. I ignored the screaming that was going on in my head. I ignored the fact that she was my best friend's little sister. I. Ignored. It. All. Nothing, and I repeat nothing, could have prepared me for what came out of her mouth next. "Hey, I need you to do me a huge favor." She leaned on the bar and then took my bottle of beer from my hand, bringing it to her mouth. At that point, so many things were going through my head. She wants me to lie about seeing her. She wants me to drive her home so she can drink. She wants me to pretend that I don't know her. I mean, the scenarios were endless. But nothing, and I mean nothing, could have prepared me for what she said next. "Can we have sex?"

I pour the coffee in the cup and laugh at the memory. I was both shocked and aroused. Also, I told her no right away. I take a sip of the coffee and head over to the couch, grabbing my iPad. I put the coffee down on the side table and look around at the almost empty house. It's coming along for sure, but I've been dragging my feet waiting for Presley to add her touch to it. Even without her knowing, I smile when I think about her. Every single part of me is in love with her.

I've known her for almost my whole life, having been best friends with her older brother, Travis, since kindergarten. When it was time to go off to college, I had no idea what I wanted to do, unlike Travis, who knew for sure what he wanted to do. So I applied to the community college, and I took a pre-law course for fun. You know what they say, that you know when you know. Well, the minute I was in that class, I knew. I knew that I wanted to learn the law. So I jumped in with both feet. Did I think I would drown? I did. Did I tell myself that no matter how many extra courses I had to take and that no matter how long it took, I would succeed? You bet your fucking ass I did. I got my bachelor's in four years and then went to law school for the next three years. It was the hardest thing I've ever had to do, and it showed me what determination and dedication meant. For seven years, I had one goal in mind and one goal only. I studied my ass off for the bar, and the minute I got the results, I got shit-faced and then ended the night with Presley in my arms. It was one of the highlights of my life. When I think about all of the highlights, she's a part of them in some way or another.

All my hard work paid off when I got offered a position at Coco & Associates right after I passed the bar. I was there for six years until I decided it was time to come back home six months ago. It also helped that they offered me partner, which I didn't have, while they courted me, so it was a no-brainer.

I mean, it's not like I didn't come home at all. In the beginning, it was less, but then when Travis almost got married years ago, I started to come back more and more. Each time I was home, Presley and I would just migrate to each other. Neither of us wanted to put a name on what we were doing. We would see each other in secret, and I didn't really care as long as I got to spend my time with her. But now that I'm back full-time, and this is where we both live, it's getting to be a thorn in my side.

My phone beeps, and I reach over and grab it, seeing it's a text from her.

Gorgeous: Umm, did you eat my panties?

I laugh, getting up and going to the couch to grab them. I hold them up on my finger to snap a picture of them. Then I send it to her.

Me: Is this what you were looking for?

Gorgeous: Yes, where were they?

Me: If you come back, I will give them back to you.

Gorgeous: Throw them out.

I can't help the laugh that comes out of me. This woman drives me crazy, and when I try to FaceTime her, she declines the call.

Gorgeous: I'm working out and all sweaty.

Me: You got pretty sweaty last night, and I was okay with it.

Gorgeous: I'm blocking you. Go away.

Me: So you don't want your panties back?

Gorgeous: I'll get them tonight.

Me: Ohh, admitting that we are having dinner together so early in the day. IT'S A MIRACLE.

Gorgeous: I'm blocking you.

Me: Have a great day, gorgeous.

Putting my phone down, I get up and walk up the steps to slip on my basketball shorts and a T-shirt before rushing out the door. I park behind her and get out of the car, rushing up her front steps. I press her doorbell and wait for her to answer. My head is down when she opens the door, and when I look up, I can't help but smile. "Hey, gorgeous." She tries not to smile as she shakes her head from side to side. Her hair is tied high on her head in a bun. Her face is red as she pants, trying to catch her breath. She's wearing a sports bra and booty shorts that should be illegal. "I came to return your panties," I say, taking a step in and wrapping one hand around her waist.

"Is that so?" she says while I pick her up, and she wraps her legs around my waist.

"That is so," I say, my lips finding hers as I carry her up the stairs to her bedroom. I suck her neck once before throwing her on her bed. "Just one problem." She gets on her elbows, looking at me. "I forgot them at home." My hands go to her hips as I peel her shorts off. Her bare pussy makes my semi-hard cock come fully awake.

"Don't you even think about it." She rolls off the bed. "I need to shower first." She looks over her shoulder as she walks to her bathroom. "Are you coming?"

"You fucking know it," I say, taking two steps, then grabbing her hips and putting my hard, covered cock up against her ass. "I'm going to be coming in more ways than one."

Three

Presley

"So what do you think?" Clarabella walks into my office, and I look away from the computer screen where I was scheduling two more meetings for tomorrow. She stands there in a pink skirt and ivory silk button-down shirt, her hip cocked to the side.

"I mean, if you are going to try anal." I lean back in my chair. "I say go for it. It hurts and is not worth the hype. But everyone is different."

"What the hell are you talking about?" she shrieks, throwing her hands in the air. Shelby comes waltzing into the room wearing black pants and a white shirt pulled up at the sleeves.

"Clarabella is thinking of trying anal." I fill Shelby in.

Her face grimaces, and she shakes her head.

"Oooh," Shelby starts. "You need to get super drunk. And then you just think you're a porn star. But then the reality is you're really not. So it's going to hurt like a motherfucker."

"Oh my God!" Clarabella yells, throwing her hands in the air. "What is wrong with you two?"

"You were the one who asked." I point at her, and she just shakes her head and puts her hands on her head.

"I was asking you about the Taylor Swift song," she says, and my eyebrows pinch together. I guess with the look on my face, she knows that I have absolutely no idea what she's talking about. "I texted you all last night," she huffs.

"Oh, that," I say, picking up my phone. "I didn't read it." They both gasp. "What? I'm learning to disconnect at night." They both tilt their head to the side. It's also because when the phone did alert me, I was in the middle of having the first orgasm of the night, but I won't add that in there.

"Disconnect?" Shelby asks with her mouth hanging open in shock. "Disconnect." She repeats the word as if she's not sure she said it out loud.

"Hold the phone," Clarabella says. "You gave me shit last month when I missed a call from you."

"It was an emergency!" I shriek, holding my hands up. "The groom literally wanted everyone to dye their hair blond because he wanted it to look like the Cullens were in attendance." My voice goes louder. "Now give me a second to look and see what we are really discussing since you didn't mean anal."

"Oh, for the love of God," Clarabella retorts.

"Why don't we just have this meeting now?" Shelby asks, going to sit down. "What happened?"

"Oh my God, you didn't read my text either?" She looks over at Shelby.

"She was probably practicing how to be a porn star." I laugh at my own joke.

"I was riding something," she says, and I can't help but gasp. "Oh, please, like you haven't ridden anything in the last six months." She rolls her eyes, and my palms start to sweat as I try to take the focus off myself and the questions that I'm sure they are dying to ask me but won't.

"Thank God I wasn't stranded on the side of the road," Clarabella declares. "Or worse off. You two were my one phone call from jail."

"You would call Travis before you called either of us." I laugh. "Because he wouldn't ask you a million questions as to why you were there."

"This is true," Shelby says. "Why would you be arrested to begin with?"

I open the text now. "Shall I read this out loud to save everyone from guessing what this important discussion was about?"

"Yes." Shelby smiles. "Save me the time of reading it."

I look down at the text message. "Have you guys heard the ten-minute song from Taylor Swift?"

Looking over at Shelby, I answer, "I have not."

"Ten-minute song?" Shelby asks, shocked. "Who the fuck has that time?" She looks over at Clarabella.

"I listened to it going home the other day." Clarabella shrugs. "And then I got sucked down the rabbit hole about who the song was about."

"Who's the song about?" I ask, not sure why I'm suddenly intrigued by this.

"Jake Gyllenhaal," Clarabella shares, looking at both me and Clarabella. "Apparently, they dated when Taylor was nineteen."

"Wait, isn't she like thirtysomething now?" Shelby grabs her phone, no doubt opening Google.

"She's thirty-two now," Clarabella informs us. "Anyway, she left a scarf at his sister's house, and she never got it back."

"Let me get this straight." I hold up my hand. "She dated him over ten years ago and has now made a ten-minute song about it."

"Yes," Clarabella says.

"She can afford another scarf," Shelby declares, and I nod, agreeing with her.

"It's not about the scarf!" Clarabella shouts. "It's about him keeping it."

"She needs to get over the fucking scarf," Shelby says.

"You know who is probably looking for that scarf." I look at both my sisters. "Jake's new girlfriend." They both laugh. "She is the only one who is walking around the fucking house saying, where the fuck is that scarf?"

"Facts," Clarabella says. "Why keep it? Isn't it bad karma?"

"Maybe it was cashmere," Shelby reasons, getting up. "Whatever it was, I'm fucking happy I didn't waste my time answering that fucking text message."

"Same," I say at the same time that the phone buzzes in my hand and the front door chimes, letting us know that someone just walked in. "That is my three o'clock." I get up from my desk. "Is my lipstick still on?"

"Yes." Clarabella nods. I walk out of my office and toward the waiting room, seeing my bride and groom. They are both looking around the room at some of the sample flower arrangements we have out.

"Hello," I greet, smiling and walking to the bride first. I've learned that you always, and I mean always, go to the woman first so she doesn't think you are trying to get her man. "I'm Presley." I hold out my hand for her.

"I'm Jenna," she replies with a smile, extending her hand to me. "This is my fiancé, Robert," she says of the groom who now turns around and smiles at me, extending his hand. The smell of his cologne is so strong my stomach lurches.

"Nice to meet you," he says to me, and I just smile. Breathing in through my mouth and not my nose.

"Shall we take a walk outside?" I suggest, trying to get out of this closed space. "So we can see the grounds, and then we can take a walk to the venue space." They look at each other and then nod at me. "If you will follow me," I say, turning to lead the way out. The hot air does nothing about the smell. My stomach feels like it's moving up to my throat. "You will see that we have chances for pictures over here." I start pitching the venue.

After doing this so many times, it's like a script, but the whole time I'm just trying to breathe easy and not barf all over the place.

"It's very pretty," Jenna observes, looking at Robert as they share a smile. I keep a smile on my face at the same time that the wind blows, and I get another whiff of his cologne.

"If you guys will just give me a minute," I say, turning and walking back up the steps as fast as I can. "Shelby!" I shout her name as soon as I walk inside, running to the desk and grabbing the garbage can right before I lose my breakfast.

"Oh my God." I hear Clarabella rushing to me as the wave of vomit comes again.

Tears are filling my eyes, and all I can do is point at the door toward where I left the couple.

"Got it," Shelby confirms, walking out and leaving me with Clarabella.

"I'll get you water," Clarabella says and all I can do is close my eyes before I throw up again.

"Oh my God, what did you eat?" Clarabella opens the top and hands me the bottle. I rinse out my mouth, spitting into the garbage before taking a sip.

"Bagel and cream cheese," I say, sitting on the floor now but not moving away from the garbage bin.

"Maybe the cheese wasn't good," Clarabella suggests.

"I was fine until Rico Suave out there came in bathed in Abercrombie and Fitch cologne," I share, my stomach lurching just from thinking about it.

"Well, whatever it is, you should go home," Clarabella

states. "I'll go get your purse and stuff."

"Thank you," I say, grabbing my phone and texting Bennett.

Me: How are you feeling?

I send the text and close my eyes to fight back the nausea when the phone beeps in my hand.

Bennett: Better now that you texted. Why?

Me: No reason.

"Here you go." Clarabella comes out with my purse and my garbage can. "And I called Mom and she said if it was the cream cheese, you would have known right away because it would have tasted sour."

"Why the hell would you call Mom?" I huff, standing up now.

"You are her baby. Can you imagine if I didn't call her?" She shakes her head. "I'm not dealing with that. I have enough to deal with. Now call me when you get home."

"Whatever," I say, grabbing my bag and the garbage bag. The minute I take two steps, I get another whiff of the cologne, and I groan and rush out to my car.

I start the car and get the air-conditioning going before pulling up my phone and googling why the fuck I'm throwing up cream cheese. I scan the list, and it's the basic lactose intolerance. I roll my eyes when I see pregnancy. Then snort-laugh at that thought. *"As if,"* I say, opening my period calculator app on my phone. The red dot in the middle says DAY 4. "No, no, no, no, no," I say, my heart beating so fast I can't hear anything else but the echo.

I throw my phone down on the passenger seat, the nausea not even on my mind as I make my way to the pharmacy. My head is spinning around and around, and I literally feel like I'm not in my own body. Parking, I grab my purse and head into the pharmacy. I speed walk down the aisles, not even sure where one finds pregnancy tests. I spot them above the condoms, and I look around before grabbing two boxes in one hand and then adding three more of other brands.

I make no eye contact when I pay for them, and the drive home has to be the longest drive of my life. It's almost like I'm going forward but taking fifteen steps backward. My neck burns, and my hands shake and get clammy. I don't even grab anything from the car but the pharmacy bag and the keys. Every single step to the bathroom feels like my feet are filled with cement. "This isn't happening," I say to myself, spilling the boxes on the bathroom counter. I pick up a box and start to read the instructions. "I need to pee," I mumble, walking to the toilet and then walking back to grab a test. "But if one is defective, how am I going to pee again?" I have a conversation with myself when I see the glass on the counter. "I'm going to pee in the cup and then dunk the tests in them." My heart feels like it's going to come out of my mouth. "Then I'm going to spin it and play Russian roulette." If I wasn't so fucking scared, this would make me laugh.

I sit on the toilet and wait for the pee to come, but when I think it will, I get bladder shy. Getting up, I walk over to the sink and turn on the water to get the urge to pee, but when I sit down, it goes away. "You better fucking pee." I look at my vagina. "And you better not be with a baby." I start to pee and then rush to put the glass in the stream. "I promise if this is negative, I will not have sex again without using double protection." I put the cup down on the floor and wipe myself. "At least no sex during ovulation," I add to the verbal contract I'm doing with whoever is listening. "Okay." I put the cup on the counter. "This looks like normal pee. Nothing looks pregnant." I laugh as I open all the boxes and start to put the sticks in the cup of urine. "Okay, three minutes." I look around for my phone and then realize I had forgotten it in the car. "Or I count to one hundred and eighty," I say, walking back and forth in my bathroom and counting to one eighty. "Here we go." I grab one and look down at the test. "Oh, fuck."

Four

Bennett

I press the disconnect button when I hear her voice mail come on. Putting the phone down, I see that it's just after four, so she might be in a meeting. I open the last text she sent me when she asked me if I felt okay. "Here are the files you asked for." Andrew, my assistant, comes in, handing me the manila folder. "Don't forget you have the weekly meeting in fifteen minutes."

"Thank you." I nod at him, opening the folder and scanning it. Fifteen minutes later, I'm walking into the conference room for the partners' weekly meeting. "Gentlemen," I say, sitting down and grabbing a bottle of water. The meeting goes on for over two hours, and when I get back to my desk, I see that she hasn't called me back. It's not that weird, but usually, she would send a text with the word Busy.

Picking up my phone, I dial her number again, and it rings four times and then goes to voice mail. I smile when I hear her voice. "You've reached Presley Baker. I'm not able to take your call right now. Please leave me a message, and I'll get back to you as soon as I can."

"Hey, gorgeous, it's me. Call me back," I say, hanging up the phone and then texting her.

Me: Are you okay?

"I'm going to head out." Andrew sticks his head into my office. "Unless you need anything."

"I think I'll be good," I tell him. "Big plans this weekend?" When I came to the firm, I started with a female assistant. She was new to the firm, and she got a little bit too good at her job. Plus, she was giving off vibes that she wanted to be more than just my assistant. She would bring lunch in for us, and it just got to the point where I knew that if I didn't cut it now, it would get worse. So we had her transferred to another department, and she quit two weeks later. As soon as that happened, I knew that my next assistant would be a male to make it safe for everyone. When Andrew came in, we just clicked. The one thing that I liked about him was that he left his problems at the door.

"We have a wedding out of town," he says with a smile. "She's waiting for me downstairs."

"You should have told me." I lean back in my chair. "Get out of here."

"Thank you." He nods politely.

"Why don't you take Monday off also?" He looks at me shocked. "You've been working long hours. You deserve it."

"I won't say no." He puts his hands in his pockets. "But only if you're sure."

"I'm sure." I nod at him.

"Have a great weekend," he says right before he turns and walks out of the door.

I pick the phone back up, wondering if she texted me back, and she hasn't. I check my emails one more time before closing everything up and leaving. Grabbing my keys and phone, I walk out, and the thick air greets me right away. The sun is setting as I start the car. I give it a couple of seconds for the air-conditioning to kick in before I leave. I start heading to my house, then turn around, and before I know it, I'm heading to Presley's work. The parking lot is empty, so I make my way over to her house, calling her once more and still getting her voice mail. *What the fuck?* I think, and I get this sense of dread that runs through me.

I speed halfway there, and when I see her car in the driveway, I take a deep breath, sighing with relief, knowing she's okay. I walk up the steps and press the doorbell instead of just barging in. I listen to see if I hear her footsteps, and I don't know if it's just me, but it feels like an eternity by the time she opens the door. But in reality, it must have been ten seconds. My head flies up to her face with a smile on it, and then my heart stops when I see her face. "What happened?" I ask her. Her eyes are red from crying, her nose is also red, and the light in her eyes is gone. "Are you sick?"

"I guess you can call it that," she says, turning around and walking inside the house. She is wearing shorts and a tank top, her black hair, which is always perfect, is piled on top of her head.

"What do you mean I can call it that?" I shut the door behind me and walk to the living room with her. I look around and see that all the drapes are closed, and the television is off. "Did someone die?"

"You can call it that," she says, sitting on the couch and folding her legs under her.

I put my hands on my hips, and my blood pressure is going through the roof. The tightness in my chest gets tighter and tighter. "Gorgeous," I say between clenched teeth. I can't remember the last time we disagreed about something. I mean, we bicker, but after like five minutes, I'm over it and just want to kiss her anyway. "You are really…"

"We need to talk," she says, and when she looks at me, I can see the turmoil in her eyes. I can tell that whatever she has to tell me is bad. I can also tell that whatever she has to tell me she doesn't know how to tell me. My heart sinks to my feet.

"Oh my God," I say in a whisper. "You're seeing someone else." My mouth goes dry at the question as the pain in my chest comes on full force. Yes, we aren't technically "dating" because I don't want to put a label on it, or else, I know she's going to freak out, but that is the first thing that came to my mind. I shake my head, trying to clear the image of her and someone else out of my brain. The left side of my arm starts to twitch, and I put my hand to my chest, thinking maybe this is me having a heart attack. "Do you smell burnt toast?" I ask her. Maybe I'm having a stroke.

"Really?" she says, rolling her eyes. "That's the first thing that comes to your mind?"

"I have no idea what to think since you aren't giving me anything." I throw my hands up in the air. "You're sitting there with tears in your eyes. You have no light in your eyes. You haven't made one snarky remark about me showing up here without calling. It's the only thing that came to mind."

"When would I have time to see someone else?" she asks me. "We literally sleep together every night."

"Not every night," I remind her, thinking of the nights she leaves me because heaven forbid we get used to each other.

"I threw up today," she tells me. I take a step to her, and she holds up her hand to stop me.

"Are you okay now?" I look around to see if maybe she needs something. "Do you want me to get you water?" I ask. The beating of my heart picks up again just as I walk over to the kitchen and open her fridge. "Did you want maybe some Gatorade?"

"Ugh," she says, putting her head back on the back of the couch.

"Are you going to be sick?" I ask her and then look at her. "Why don't you have a bucket around in case you throw up? Do you want some soup?" I ask, sitting next to her now and taking my phone out of my pocket. "Maybe just the broth. I can call Luke and see if he can make you something."

"I don't think soup is going to make this better," she says softly, looking down at her lap, and I notice something white in her hand with a blue tip.

"Oh, God," I say, and she looks over at me. "You didn't go on Google again, did you?" I shake my head. "The last time you did that, you thought you had bedbugs. You were throwing your mattress out the window."

"It looked like bedbugs," she says through clenched teeth.

"It was mosquito bites," I remind her. "We went hiking."

"Bennett." She says my name and then holds up a white stick in her hand.

"What is that?" I take it from her, not sure what I'm looking at until I see the word **pregnant**. My mouth opens as I look at her. "Is this…?" My hands shake as I hold the stick. So many emotions are going through me, but the main one is my heart feels so fucking full.

"I can tell you what it's not." She blinks away the tears. "It's not a thermometer."

My heart fills my throat as I look down at the letters again. "Pregnant," I say the words again. The tears fill my eyes. "I can't." The lump in my throat makes it hard to say anything. But I can't stop the smile that fills my face. From ear to fucking ear. "We're having a baby." I lean in to her. "We're having a baby." I kiss her ever so lightly. She moves her hand up, palming my cheek.

"I don't know about the we part," she says, "but I am definitely with child."

Five

Presley

"Pregnant." He says the word, and I can see the tears filling his eyes. Which in turn makes my stomach flutter, which then makes me blame the baby. "I can't." He gets choked up, and the smile on his face is from ear to ear. "We're having a baby." My heart is pounding so hard I think it's literally going to come out of my chest. "We're having a baby." He leans in and kisses my lips softly. The nerves die down just a bit. My hand moves up on its own as I cup his cheek.

"I don't know about the we part," I say, pushing away from him and getting up. "But I am definitely with child."

"How do you know for sure?" he asks as I stand here in front of him. The shades are all closed as if I'm mourning a death.

"Well, this morning I went into work and I was fine, and then this groom came in and he smelled as if he was sixteen and just got a hold of his father's aftershave." I close my eyes and grimace at the thought. "Made me lose my breakfast." He just stares at me, and his look is just filled with so much feeling that my chest fills with something that I don't want to think about because as soon as it fills, I get this overwhelming sense of sadness. "Then I googled about the cream cheese being bad, and well, it said pregnancy, so I laughed because..."

"Because we always use protection." He sits on the couch with the pregnancy test in his hands.

"Right, but then I went on my period app." I start to pace in front of him, and all he does is sit on the couch all cool, calm, and collected. "And it was like four days ago."

"You should have called me." He gets up now. "I would have…"

"Helped me how? Pee on the stick?" I point at the stick.

"I don't know. Hold your hand," he says. "Support you."

"Besides, I was in the state of denial for a good hour after." I shake my head. My head is spinning a million miles a minute. I think I'm about to hyperventilate, but I block it all off. "It's fine." I look at him. "I'm pregnant, and I go from here."

He walks over to me now, putting the stick in his pocket. His hands come up to hold my face. "Gorgeous," he says softly, "relax."

"I am relaxed," I reply, even though I'm the opposite of relaxed. I'm to the point that I'm freaking the fuck out, but even more so because I thought he would be freaking out with me. "You're a lot more relaxed than I thought you would be."

"What does that mean?" he asks, and I just look at him.

"It means that we went from exchanging orgasms to now me being pregnant," I say, and I have to move away from his touch because if I don't, I'm afraid that he's going to see exactly what I'm feeling and I'm never going to let that happen. I just can't.

"We shared a lot more than orgasms, gorgeous." His lips find mine, and the beating in my chest slows down. "And we are going to be sharing a lot more from now on."

"I don't even know what else there is to share with you." I laugh. "I mean, you've already taken my virginity, and now you've planted a baby in me." He throws his head back and laughs, and I can't help but lean in and kiss his neck. "I have to tell my sisters."

"Okay," he says. "What time are they coming over?"

I push him away from me. "You are not going to be here when they come here."

"Why not?" he asks, shocked as he puts his hands on his hips.

"Because," I say, walking over to the kitchen to grab an apple juice, which I never drink, "I'm going to tell them."

"Okay," he says. "But I'm telling your brother."

I laugh. "You really think that is a good idea?"

He shrugs his shoulders. "It's not a surprise that I'm into you."

"Oh, you are in me all right." I grab the glass and wink at him. "You left a couple of things in me as we speak."

I grab the phone on the counter that I went into the car and got after the initial shock. "Oh, you have a phone," he says. "Funny, I kept calling."

"I was in shock." I roll my eyes. "I had five tests staring back at me telling me that I'm a plus-one."

I pull up the text thread.

Me: Hey, so this is an SOS Emergency sister meeting.

I put the phone down, and my hands shake. "This should be fun."

Clarabella: Oh, now she answers after hours.

Shelby: This better not be to discuss Taylor Swift.

Me: Trust me when I say this is an emergency.

Clarabella: Prove it.

Shelby: Why would you ask her to prove it?

Me: Code Purple.

Shelby: Fuck, on my way.

Clarabella: I'm there in four minutes.

I put the phone down. "Okay, you have to go," I urge, walking to him and grabbing his hand.

"It's going to take them longer than five seconds to get here." He laughs, and when I look at him, my vagina tenses a little bit. I didn't notice that he's wearing his dress pants, and the sleeves of his button-down shirt are rolled up to his elbows. His silver Rolex on his wrist makes him sexy as hell.

"They are going to get here in record time. I just threw down a code purple," I tell him, knowing he won't understand, and I also know that I don't have time to sit down and explain it to him. I need him to get his ass out of this house. "I'll call you later." I kiss his lips and push him out the door.

"Promises, promises." He shakes his head and walks down the stairs. "Stop staring at my ass."

"It's right in my line of sight," I tell him as he looks over his shoulder, and I hold out my hand, showing him that it's right in front of my eyes.

"I can come back and hide in your room until after, and you can touch it," he says once he gets to his car, looking at me.

"Touching it got us into this mess." I point at my stomach. "We should have done a little less touching."

He shakes his head. "Would not recommend that at all. Now that it's too late, we can do it all the time."

"We already do it all the time," I retort. "Now get out of here." I shoo him away, and I walk back inside to grab a glass of apple juice. The sweetness makes my mouth alive. I'm pouring myself another glass when I hear a car door shut. "Here we go, little one," I say, putting my hand on my stomach.

The front door opens and then shuts back with a slam. "What in the world?" I hear Shelby say as she walks in slowly. Almost like she is afraid to walk in, she finally makes it to the kitchen. "Why is it so dark in here?" she asks while she looks around. "Why are you sitting in the dark?"

I don't have a chance to answer her because I hear the shriek of brakes, and then the sound of a car door shutting. "Presley!" Clarabella yells my name, running up the steps. "This better be fucking good," she says, walking in and slamming the door. "Hello," she says, not moving from the front door. "Is anyone here?"

"There are three cars outside," Shelby says, turning on the light and then looking over at me. "Oh my God, who died?"

"Someone better have died," Clarabella says, coming into the kitchen wearing a bathrobe.

"Oh my God," I say. "Are you naked under there?"

"Yes." She nods her head. "We were…"

"If you tell me that you were in the middle of having sex," Shelby scolds, "I'm going to…"

"Who answers in the middle of having sex?" Clarabella says. "It was the pre-game."

"Oh my God." Shelby closes her eyes. "I can't get the picture out of my head."

"Well, this is going to go a lot better than I thought it was going to go," I say, and they look at me.

"You called code purple," Shelby reminds me. "It better be life or death." When we were in college, and we would go out, the code word was purple bear. If we texted your purple bear in, it meant we needed backup.

"I did," I say, my heart speeding up a bit. "Well, there is no way to say this… so."

"Are you dying?" Clarabella interrupts me, her eyes

filling with tears. "Is that why you are sitting in the dark?"

"Can you shut the fuck up?" Shelby says. "She isn't dying. She's glowing." She looks at me. "I mean, not at the moment." She does a weird face. "You look like shit, and like you're about to die, but this morning, you glowed."

"I'm pregnant." I come right out and say it. "Like ripping off the Band-Aid," I say, pouring myself another glass of apple juice and taking it like a shot.

"I'm sorry," Clarabella says, holding her robe together on top. "What did you just say?"

"You are not!" Shelby shrieks. "You can't be."

I walk over to the living room to grab the four tests that I have, turning to see Shelby walk over to the kitchen counter and pick up my cup and smell inside of it. "Don't touch it," Clarabella hisses over to her.

"I'm pregnant," I repeat. "Not filled with germs."

"I need a drink," Shelby states, walking over to the cabinet on top of the fridge, knowing that is where I keep the booze. We all keep it above the fridge like it's a secret. "Do you want one?"

"I don't know," Clarabella says. "I don't want to touch anything."

"You can't catch pregnancy," Shelby tells her.

"Forget that you know how people get pregnant… sex," Clarabella informs her, and Shelby gasps out.

"Shocking, really, is that how it happens?" Shelby mocks, grabbing the bottle and just taking a shot. "I thought the stork flies over and brings it to you."

"They probably had sex right there." Clarabella

points at her. "You are in the same spot your niece and or nephew were planted into her."

Shelby looks down at the counter and then looks over at me. "Did you do it here?"

"Oh my God," I say, walking into the kitchen and tossing one of the tests to Shelby and one to Clarabella.

"This is," Shelby says, grabbing the stick and looking down at it. "Mine says pregnant."

"So does mine," Clarabella confims to her.

"That's because I'm pregnant!" I shout. "Can we just for once focus?"

"I'm trying to focus," Clarabella says. "Who is the father?"

I fold my arms over my chest and huff out, "It's Bennett."

"Holy shit," they both say at the same time.

"We are not shocked in the least," they both say together. "Are you shocked?"

"Well, yeah," I say, throwing my hands up.

"Where does it go wrong?" Clarabella asks me while Shelby hits her shoulder. "What? I'm

asking her if she was using protection."

"Obviously, she uses protection." Shelby rolls her eyes. "You did use it, right?"

"We did each time," I tell them.

"And how many times are we talking?" Clarabella asks me while Shelby groans out and slaps the counter. "What? These are questions people ask."

"What people?" I ask them. "Who?"

"I don't know; it's not like we have a playbook on

how to act when your sister tells you they are pregnant," Clarabella says.

"Did you tell Bennett?" Shelby asks me.

"Oh, good question," Clarabella sings out. "Does he know? What did he say?"

"I just told him," I confirm to both of them.

"Well, then, why isn't he here?" Clarabella says. "Oh my God, is he hiding upstairs?" She pulls the top of her robe tighter.

"He is not here," I share, walking and grabbing the apple juice instead of the scotch.

"Why isn't he here?" Clarabella now asks, her tone tight when she cocks her hip to the side and folds her arms over her chest.

"Why does he need to be here?" I throw up my hands, ignoring the way that my stomach gets tight and my chest suddenly burns. "It's my body."

"It is," Shelby says softly. "And you get to decide what you do with your body." She shares a look with Clarabella.

"Okay, before we make rash decisions." Clarabella holds up her hands. "Can we not talk about it?" She walks over to me. "I already love it." Putting her hand on my stomach.

"It," Shelby hisses.

"Okay, one"—I hold up my finger—"I'm having the baby; there was never a question about it." I put my hand on Clarabella's. "But I'm doing this alone."

"That motherfucker," Shelby hisses out.

"Oh, he's happy. He kept saying, we are having a

baby." I shake my head, ignoring all the screaming going on in my brain. "But the reality of it is, I'm having the baby." I grab the glass, bringing it to my mouth. "And it's going to be fine."

Six

Bennett

I park my car on the street, turning it off. Looking at the house and seeing shadows from inside, I have a feeling that I should have called before coming here. Getting out of the car, I walk up the pathway toward the front door, seeing a toy truck on the side and smiling. The sound of dogs barking and utter chaos comes through the window, and I'm about to hold up my hand and knock on the door when it's pulled open. "What the hell are you doing?" Travis says to me, and I laugh.

"Normally, when someone shows up at one's door," I inform him, chuckling, "one either rings or knocks."

"Shut the fuck up," Travis says, moving away from the door. "You're family." I walk in, closing the door behind me, and I'm greeted by the two dogs they got when they got married.

"Hey, you two." I bend down to greet them. "Are you keeping out of trouble?"

"Who was it?" I hear Harlow who sticks her head out of the kitchen and smile at me.

"This idiot was at the door, and he had the audacity to try to knock," Travis informs her, shaking his head.

"Imagine that," Harlow says, coming to me now. "Having the balls to knock before storming in." She gets on her tippy-toes and kisses my cheek. "Why would you do that?"

"I just don't want to catch him naked." I motion with my head toward Travis. "I've seen him naked enough to last me a lifetime." I look over to see Travis taking his daughter out of her high chair.

"Look who came to visit," he says, taking off her bib and then wiping her face. "Uncle B." He turns and hands me Charlotte.

"Hey there, beautiful girl," I say, bending down and kissing her still wet cheek. She gets all excited and starts batting my chest.

"So what are you doing here?" Travis asks, walking to the kitchen that looks like a tornado has gone through it.

"I have to talk to you," I say, my heart speeding up, and I avoid looking at him as I look down at Charlotte.

"Oh, sounds like you two need to be alone," Harlow says, coming to me. "I'm going to go and give Charlotte a bath." Charlotte throws herself at her mother. "And you two go and have men time outside. I'm going to put her to bed and then relax before the hellion comes home from the farm tomorrow." She mentions her son, Theo, who is going through the terrible twos and making sure they don't forget it.

"It's my turn for bath time," Travis says, handing me a bottle of beer.

"Last time it was bath time, it looked like a tsunami hit the bathroom," Harlow reminds him. "So you just saved me."

"Glad I could be of service," I say, grabbing the bottle of beer.

"Let's go sit outside," Travis suggests, and I suddenly get nervous about what is to come. We've been best friends since kindergarten. He's the brother that I've never had, and I know that if I call him, regardless of the time or the situation, he would be there beside me and I to him also.

"This is nice," I say, looking around at the patio that they just had done, which opens up into a huge yard with a play structure.

"My father-in-law." He sits down on one of the couches. "Came over one weekend, and the next thing you know, I'm looking outside, and he has this crew of fifty." His father-in-law is what you call a cowboy. He has all these farms, but not only is he a cowboy and you don't want to fuck with him, he's a computer wizard. It's the strangest thing I've ever seen. I think someone even said something that he trained with the SEALs for fun. Who does that?

I laugh, sitting on the couch beside him. "Let me guess, did you come outside to help?" I take a pull of my beer.

His eyebrows pinch together. "Are you out of your mind?" he huffs. "He had shovels and shit. You think I was going to come out here so I can give him a reason to actually bury me?"

I can't help but laugh at that, and I'm glad that I swallowed the beer, or I would have spit it out. "He doesn't still hate you," I tell him. "You gave him two grandkids."

"I broke her heart and left her for four years," he reminds me. "And I was going to marry someone else."

"Yeah, you can spin lots of things." I shake my head. "But no matter what, you are never going to live that down."

"Exactly," he says and then looks at me. "What's on your mind?"

I chuckle and take a pull of beer before I break the news to him. I'm both nervous and excited. "I'm going to be a father." I start with the easiest thing. Just saying the words, I can't help but smile big. The fullness that I feel is out of this world, and I didn't even know something was missing before now.

"Shut up," Travis says, shocked as he looks at me. "I mean…" He puts his arm around my neck, and his hand squeezes my shoulder. "I'm happy for you."

"It's Presley," I share, holding my breath, and now I'm wondering if perhaps sitting next to him wasn't the smartest idea.

"Wait a minute." His hand moves from around my shoulder. "Presley, as in my sister Presley?"

"The one and only," I confirm, and I don't know what I'm expecting, to be honest. He could be happy for me, or he could turn around and punch me in the face for sleeping with his sister. Either way, it doesn't change the outcome of the situation.

"Oh my God," he says. "I…" He stops, looks at me, and questions, "Presley?"

"Yeah." I nod my head, and out of everything I've done in my life, this moment right here, saying that she is going to have my child, it is everything. "There is no one on this earth that I want to be with but her."

He throws his head back, and he laughs now. "Does she know this?"

I chuckle, the burning hitting my stomach now. "I'm going to marry her," I say, bringing the bottle to my lips and taking a pull.

"Is that a fact?" He can't help but throw his head back and laugh. His whole body shakes with laughter. "You told her this?" he asks me, and I just glare at him.

"She calls herself a lone wolf," I remind him. "You think she's going to be open to marrying me?"

"Not a chance," he admits to me, taking his own pull of his beer. "She's going to fight you the whole fucking way."

"Oh, I know." I smile, putting the bottle against my neck. "Trust me, I know."

"This is going to be fun to watch." He sits back on the couch and looks over at me.

"I can always use my charm." I shrug. "Made her sleep with me."

"You might lose some body parts along the way." He raises his eyebrows, and he's about to say something else when the back door opens, and Harlow comes rushing out with a naked and dripping wet Charlotte on her hip.

We both stand at the same time, expecting the house to be on fire or something else. "Oh my God," she says, holding up the phone. "Is everything okay out here?"

"Why are you rushing like a bat out of hell?" He walks over to her swiftly.

"Clarabella just called me," she says, looking at Travis and then at me. "And told me about a certain situation going on."

"Is that code for Presley being pregnant?" I ask her, and she opens her mouth in shock and then looks over at Travis to see his reaction. "I told him already."

"And everything is okay?" She looks at Travis, who reaches out to grab Charlotte.

"Everything is fine." Travis leans down and kisses her lips. "He was just telling me how he's going to marry Presley." Harlow throws her head back, similar to her husband, and laughs out loud. She also adds clapping her hands together. "See." He points at his wife.

"She's the lone wolf," Harlow reminds me, and I roll my eyes. "I mean, she says it."

"Every single time," I finish the sentence for her. "I know, I know." I hold up my hands. "But she's having my baby."

"Lots of people raise kids together without being

married," Travis reminds me.

"Well, I want to marry her. Does that say anything?" The pit of my stomach burns when they just look at each other with "that poor bastard" look. "Okay, well, this is fun." I put the bottle of beer down. "But I'm going to head out." I walk back up the steps, kissing Charlotte on the cheek. "You two," I say to Harlow and Travis. "Suck balls."

"If it's any consolation," Travis says. "I'm glad you're her baby daddy."

"Thanks, that means a lot." I put my hand to the middle of my chest over my heart. "Wish me luck."

"Oh, you are going to need a lot more than luck," Harlow warns. "But in Presley's defense, her siblings didn't help that matter." She looks at her husband. "At all."

"It's like PTSD," Travis says. "But in the end, we all ended up happy."

"Yeah, well, good to know," I say, walking past them and out the front door. I get in the car and make my way home.

The whole time all I can think about is going to her, but knowing that she is probably freaking out and the more I push myself in her face, the faster she is going to push me away.

Walking up the steps of the house, making my way through the door, and not even stopping in the kitchen, I just head straight for the living room, collapsing on the couch. The stick in my pocket slipping out and falling to the floor. I pick it up and look at it again, the smile coming to my face. "She's having our baby." I put the stick on my chest and think back to how this all started.

The knock on the door was so soft that I wasn't sure I heard it. I got up from the couch and walked over, pulling open the door. I was shocked and surprised that Presley was the one standing at my door step. I had left the bar not thirty minutes ago, after she leaned against the bar asking me the most ridiculous request. I also hightailed it out of there before I did something stupid like actually give in to her. "What are you doing here?" I asked her and stuck my head out to see if she was with anyone. "Are you here alone?"

"Yup," she said, pushing herself to come into my apartment. "Are you here alone?" She looked around the living room, my books were scattered all over the place. She placed her hands in the back pockets of her jeans and all I could do was stare at her. When did she become so fucking hot?

"Should I call Travis?" I asked her as my heart started to speed up to a not normal rhythm and I suddenly got nervous. "Or anyone else?"

"Bennett." She said my name and my cock sprang to action. It sounded like it was between a moan and a plea. "I asked you for a favor."

I groaned at that moment and looked up to the ceiling. "Oh, God, Presley, you can't be serious right now."

"Why not?" I didn't even hear her move close to me but suddenly her hands were on my hips, and all I could do was swallow because my mouth became dry. "I don't want to go to college a virgin."

"Okay, one, there is nothing wrong with you going to college a virgin," I huffed, trying to focus on the words that were coming out of my mouth and less on the way her hands felt on me. "In fact, it's even sexier."

"Please," she said in a plea. "There is no one else I want to be my first." I looked into her blue eyes and I was lost. I didn't even have time to make a decision because she got on her tippy-toes and her lips found mine.

"I'm going to make her mine," I tell the dark room when I blink away the memories. "She's always been mine. Now it's time to show her."

Seven

Presley

$\mathscr{T}$he sound of the phone beeping wakes me from my sleep and usually I would have jumped out of bed. But my eyes flutter closed and I sink deeper into the bed. "Just five more minutes." I snuggle with the covers at my neck. I'm about to slip into sleep again when I hear a soft knock on the door. "Are you kidding me." I slip my hand out of my covers and look at my watch. "Who the hell is at my door at seven freaking a.m.?" I don't know who I'm asking and I also know that no one is going to answer me. "Do you think if I ignore them, they are going to go away?" I don't wait for an answer because I hear the beeping of the front door keypad before the lock opens. "Well, that can be four people," I say to myself.

"But I'm going to go out on a limb and say that it's not anybody related to me." The room is dark with the light coming in from the open door.

"Gorgeous." I hear his voice and close my eyes, not bothering to answer him because it's a matter of time before he finds me and it's not like I'm playing hide-and-seek. "There you are," he says from the doorway of my bedroom. "This isn't like you." I hear his soft voice come closer and closer to the bed, and I open my eyes. "Usually, you are out of bed at five." He stands there in blue pants and a white button-down shirt tucked in with a brown belt. The two top buttons are open and I can already taste his skin under my lips. Usually, I see him at the end of the day with his sleeves rolled up but now with them down he looks so official, and handsome as hell.

"I know," I huff when he sits on the side of the bed. "But I literally could not drag my ass out of bed." He puts his arm over me and leans in to kiss my lips. My stomach flutters as I push away the thought that I actually missed him last night. I also ignore that I was surprised that he didn't come over or the fact that I was sad that he didn't.

"I brought you breakfast," he says and the minute he says that, my stomach lets out a big grumble and he laughs. "Looks like I'm right on time. Why don't I go grab the food and bring it to you?" He moves his hand up and down my side.

"What did you get?" I ask him, not even caring at this point, I could eat a house. When did I become so hungry?

"I got you some pancakes, eggs, French toast, and

some fruit," he says and all I can do is smile at him. "Does that smile mean I did good?" He leans in again to give me a kiss and I bask in it.

"You did good," I tell him as he gets up and I toss the covers off me, showing him that I was sleeping naked.

"Damn," he says, looking at me up and down slowly. "Maybe I can have breakfast myself." The way his voice comes out makes my knees weak.

"Let me see how good breakfast is and then maybe we can both have dessert." I walk into the bathroom, knowing that he's looking at me. I brush my teeth and go the bathroom, grabbing my white robe he bought me. I look in the mirror, making sure that I don't look like I just crawled out of bed. I also take a second and look at my stomach again. I spent most of last night standing by the mirror, looking at it from the front and the side to see if maybe there was a clue there that I was pregnant. There was nothing there, nothing. My stomach was still flat, and when I walk out, he's walking back in with my big tray. "How much food did you get?"

"Well, considering you are eating for two." He smirks and his eyes light up. "A lot." He stops, waiting for me to get back in bed. "Why did you put your robe on?"

I laugh at him. "Because I'm going to be eating." I prop the pillows behind my back and look down at all the food he's brought me. He places the tray on my lap and walks over to his side and gets in the bed on top of the covers.

"So, what are you going to eat first?" he says, grabbing a strawberry and biting into it and then offering me the other piece. I open my mouth and take it and the sweetness hits my tongue. "Did you call the doctor?" he asks me and I look at him annoyed now.

"It's been twelve hours," I tell him, grabbing my fork and cutting the blueberry pancake he got for me.

"I know, but I don't know, should you call and make sure that everything is okay?" he asks me and I avoid looking at him. "How far along are we?"

"I'm assuming I'm about five weeks." I avoid how my heart beat different when he said the *we*.

"We should call and set up an appointment," he says between bites.

"We shouldn't," I say, taking another bite of the pancake. "I should."

I look over at him and he just stares at me and my heart speeds up in my chest. "Don't you have work to get to?"

"Is that your way of telling me to shut up?" he asks me, and I want to reach over and run my hand through his hair. His perfectly styled black hair, but instead of doing what I want to do, I turn back and eat my breakfast. "I told Travis."

"I heard," I tell him, grabbing some fruit. "Harlow said you were over there."

"What did your sisters say?" he asks me and I laugh.

"They were surprised," I admit to him.

"What about when you told them I was the father?" he asks me and I say nothing. "You did tell them I was the father." He sits up now and I can't hold in the laughter anymore.

"I mean, I tried to tell them it was Jason Momoa." I try not to smile. "But they didn't believe me."

He puts his cup down on the side table and turns back to me. "Are you done?" He moves the tray off me, getting off the bed and putting the tray of food on the dresser. I watch him the whole time. Everything about him makes my knees weak; it's always been him. Always, from the first time I could never even think of being with anyone else. "So, what are you going to do today?" He sits next to me with his feet on the floor as he leans over me, his lips close to mine.

"I'm going to go to work," I say, running my hands through his hair just like I wanted to do when he walked into the room. "I have a wedding today." I look over and see that I'm already late and I should bust my ass to get out of bed. But I give myself a couple more minutes.

"You"—he bends and kisses my neck on the right side—"are going to call the doctor." He kisses the left side now and I move my neck to give him access. His kisses make me forget everything. "And then you are going to call me." He kisses my lips. "Right, gorgeous?"

My eyes flutter open now. "Are you going to persuade me?" I lean up to kiss him, my whole chest getting full.

"No." He gets up. "You have to get up and get going and I won't have enough time with you."

"Um." I get on my elbows. "It can be only about me."

"It's always about you." He bends once more and kisses me. "But I don't have enough time. Then you are going to be rushing to get out of here and then blame me for being late."

"Fine," I huff. "Then get going or else I'm going to be late."

"Always pushing me out." He smiles at me, leaning down, and rubbing his nose with mine. "You'll call me, right?" He kisses me one more time and I ignore him. He gives me one more second before he says, "Gorgeous."

"Ugh, fine." I throw the covers off me. "I'll call you, now get out."

"Have a good day, gorgeous," he says one more time before walking out. I listen to his feet walk out the door. I move over to the curtain and sneak looking outside as I watch him walk to the car. My heart starts to speed up, just like it always does, and then when he gets in the car and looks up, my heart suddenly sinks in my chest. I fight away the tears that threaten to come but I'm not fast enough this morning, or maybe it's the hormones in my body. The single tear rolls down my cheek. My heart hurts thinking that I can't give him what he needs. Thinking that he deserves someone who is going to love him without all the doubt going off in my head. Thinking that eventually he isn't going to be kissing me awake in the morning. Thinking back to my brother and sisters and seeing what happened to them the first time they tried to find their significant other. Knowing it never worked out and the second time was the charm.

I put my hand to my chest as I think about Bennett being my first everything. He's been my first crush, my first time in bed, the first man I've loved, and knowing that the first one never ever works out. Knowing the history and knowing that I should have let him go before makes me hate myself even more. Knowing that I should have cut this out years ago, but one look from him and I forget it all. One touch and I'm a puddle in his hand.

I walk to the bathroom numb, my head spins, and just like every other time I try to tell myself that it's going to be okay. But it's so much more this time. We are having a baby. A baby. I put my hand to my stomach. "No matter what, he's going to love you forever." The tears roll down my cheeks. "He'll be forever your first love." I smile through the tears now. "He'll be forever our first love."

Eight

Bennett

$\int$ pick up the phone the minute I get in the car and text her, pulling her name up and smiling as I type the sentence out.

Me: *How is everything going?*

Putting the phone in the cupholder, I start the car and drink the rest of my protein shake. My chest is rising and falling as I try to get my breathing down to a normal rate. I just spent the last two hours in the gym pushing myself until my arms felt like noodles and my knees were going to give out on me. The phone beeps now, telling me that I have a message and I see her name flash on the center screen.

Gorgeous: Uneventful. Bride showed up, groomed

showed up, so they are already winning.

I laugh.

Me: What time are you going to be done?

I look at the clock and see it's just a little bit after eight.

Gorgeous: I should be out of here in about an hour. I'm exhausted.

Me: I can come and get you if you want.

Gorgeous: No, I'm okay to drive.

Me: Okay, come over and I'll cook for you.

Gorgeous: I should go home and take a bath.

Me: Or you can come over and we can take a bath together.

Gorgeous: What are you going to cook me?

Me: Whatever you want.

Gorgeous: Shrimp pasta.

I put my head back; of course she would pick something I have no idea how to cook.

Gorgeous: What's the matter, cat got your tongue? HA HA

Me: Not at all. See you in an hour.

Instead of going straight home, I pull up the best shrimp pasta recipe that I can find online; well, the best according to the stars and reviews. Parking my car, I rush into the grocery store, grabbing everything on the list, along with a can of whipped cream. I also grab some candy and chocolate along with some chips. By the time I walk out of the grocery store and make my way back to my car, the basket is now full. I don't even notice that I was in the store for forty-five minutes and when I get home we arrive at the same time.

I get out of my car and walk over to hers, pulling open her driver's side door. She looks up at me smiling as I extend my hand to her. "Hey, gorgeous." She slips her hand in mine and puts one foot out and I see she is wearing her white stiletto heels. She grabs her bag with her free hand, standing up. Her hair is loose and curled at the end and I want nothing more than to bury my hands in it.

"Hi." She smiles and I let go of her hand and wrap it around her waist.

"You smell so good," I say, burying my face in her neck and kissing her.

"I wish I could say the same." She laughs and pushes me away, but I don't let go of her waist. Instead, I pull her even closer to me. Her chest is against mine and she puts her hands on my bare arms. I look down at the gray T-shirt that I'm wearing and the basketball shorts I threw on when I got to the gym.

"I was going to shower when I got home." I kiss her lips. "But then someone wanted shrimp. If I knew that it would take me this long, I would have showered at the gym."

"If it makes you feel any better." She doesn't move her hands from my arms. "I'm really, really hungry. Clarabella brought me a slider and just the look of it made my stomach lurch."

"How does that make me feel better?" I let her go and grab her hand as we walk back to my car and I pop the trunk with my free hand. "It makes me feel even worse, since it'll take forty-five minutes minimum to cook." I open the trunk and she gasps out as she sees it's full.

"What the hell is all this?" She looks at all the bags.

"I stopped to get stuff for the recipe," I admit. "And then, well, I ended up going down all the aisles, quickly grabbing what I thought you might want to snack on."

"Is that whipped cream?" She lets go of my hand and grabs the bottle of whipped cream that is sticking out of the bag.

"I don't know if maybe you had a sweet tooth." I wink at her as she laughs. "The last time we had one of that."

"I was sticky for two days," she reminds me.

"No." I shake my head. "That was the honey and chocolate."

"Oh, yeah." She looks up at me and her eyes shine and I love this side of her. The side where she lets down the wall that she has up. The side that shows me how much she cares. The side that is soft yet vulnerable. The side that if she knew she was showing me, she would deny. She would also put up the wall that she always has up, and I don't know what I would have to do to knock it back down. "You really do love eating things off me."

"I'm not the only one." I laugh, grabbing the bag. "You started with the chocolate."

"That was you." She gasps out and points at me. "I was following your lead."

"Let me get you inside and off your feet," I tell her as she leans in to grab one of the bags. "Don't you think about it, Presley Baker." I say her full name and it feels weird not calling her gorgeous.

"Oh, you know he's pissed when he says my name," she jokes with me and lets go of the bag. "Fine, I'll just sit and make you cater to me." She tilts her head back and I take advantage of it and kiss her lips.

"That sounds like a great plan," I agree with her and watch her walk in front of me. The green pants she is wearing mold to her ass and all I want to do is bite it. The sage-green-striped, quarter-length, long-sleeved silk shirt with cuffs is tucked in. Knowing Presley, she has matching bra and panties under it.

She unlocks the door for me and turns on the light at the entrance, as she kicks off her shoes in the corner and walks in tossing her bag on the table in the hallway. I walk past her to the kitchen, dumping the bags on the white island, and going back out to grab the rest. When I come back in, she's in the kitchen putting away stuff. "I'm going to snack on some fruits," she tells me, walking over to the sink and rinsing off the raspberries I bought. "And then I'm going to have ten chips."

I place the rest of the bags on the counter. "Everything in moderation." She tosses a raspberry in her mouth and moans. "Those are so sweet." She grabs a couple more.

"Here, let me taste," I say, walking to her and instead of grabbing one from the container, I put my arms around her waist and bend my head so that my lips can find hers. My tongue comes out and slides with hers. The kiss starts off slow but then she drops the container of raspberries on the counter and wraps her arms around me. I move my head from one side to the other, making the kiss deepen, and if her stomach didn't growl out at that moment, I would have carried her upstairs to the shower with me.

"Okay, that is my cue," I say, letting go of her lips, "to feed you." I give her a soft kiss before my arms drop from her waist but stop at her ass. I pull her tighter to me and she feels that my cock is hard and ready.

"Or," she says but her stomach cuts in again.

"I'm going to go shower," I tell her. "And then I'll start cooking."

"Ugh, fine," she says, grabbing another raspberry at the same time that she opens the bag of chips. "I wonder if raspberry and barbecue chips taste good together."

"I'll leave you to try that," I say, jogging upstairs. Kicking off my shoes as soon as I walk through the master bedroom and into the walk-in closet right before the bathroom. I peel the shirt off me and toss it in the basket in the corner, along with the shorts and boxers. My cock is still wondering what is going on when I get in the shower. I shower in record time, knowing that she's downstairs and feel this guilt that I'm starving my child at the same time.

I grab a pair of black basketball shorts before going back downstairs. I can see the kitchen is cleaned the second I make my way down the steps. The food has been put away and she sits on the couch watching television. The bag of barbecue chips beside her along with empty container of what was the raspberries. "Hey," I say and she looks over at me, and instead of going to the kitchen, I walk to her and bend to kiss her lips. I taste salt now. "You good?"

"I finished all the raspberries and ate more than ten chips." She shrugs.

"I'm sure it's going to be fine." I laugh and kiss her one more time.

"You smell good." She kisses my jaw. "Clean and fresh." I laugh, getting up and walking over to the kitchen counter and grabbing my phone and pulling up the recipe.

I start grabbing the things I need and look over to see her getting up and coming over to the kitchen. She walks behind me and puts her hands on my hips. "You look sexy." She kisses my back and I laugh.

"Do I look sexy because I'm cooking you food?" I ask her over my shoulder and her eyes light up even more as she tries not to laugh. "That's what I thought."

She can't help but laugh now. "You always look sexy," she tells me. "Like when you wear a suit."

I groan out. "I hate wearing suits," I remind her. I really do. I've always hated it, but I love what I do, so I dress the part.

"I know you do, which makes it even sexier," she says. "You looked especially sexy this morning."

"Is that so?" I focus on the recipe, even though my cock wants me to turn around and place her on the counter so I can fuck her.

"That is so and now"—her hands run up my stomach and it literally sucks in—"it's even sexier."

"You know what is going to be even sexier?" I say to her and she winks at me. "Not that. Making you dinner."

"Ugh, fine," she says. "We can talk and make a plan."

I know the minute she gets her wall back up because her body goes stiff. Her hands fall from me and straight to her sides.

"What plan is this?" She avoids looking at me as she walks around the counter toward the stool in front of me.

"Well, we have to talk about telling our parents." I look at her. "We need to get in with the doctor as soon as possible and we." She holds up her hand and I can tell she's annoyed.

"All this we we we," she says and I look at her. "I'm the one having the baby."

"And you are the one having the baby." I try to keep calm instead of losing my shit. "But that is my child also." I point at her. "You aren't doing this alone."

Nine

Presley

"And you are the one having the baby." He looks at me and I can see the vein in his neck start to pulse and I know that he's trying not to freak out. "But that is my child also." He points at me. "You aren't doing this alone." The lump goes from my stomach to my throat. "You can be carrying the baby and nurturing it," he says, looking back down at what he is doing in front of him. "And I can never tell you how much that means to me." His voice goes soft at the end.

"I'm not doing it just for you," I say, rolling my eyes.

"I can't do anything for the next eight months," he says. "The only thing I can do is make sure that you are taken care of." His words make my heart speed up. "The only thing that I can do is make you happy." He shrugs. "I mean, I've always wanted you to be happy regardless of *us*"—he emphasizes the word us—"having a baby *together*." I try to talk myself off the ledge in front of me, and then he just lays more on me. "For the rest of your life, my main concern is taking care of you both." He stares into my eyes while he says the words. "Period. That's my job. To take care of you and our children."

"Okay, one." I hold up a finger. "It's one baby, not two." He rolls his lips. "And, two." I hold up another finger. "You know I can take care of myself, right?" I point out to him and he turns to take a pan out and turn on the stove. "Like you weren't here for the last what, eight years, and I survived just fine." The way my heart is beating it's almost like it's getting ready to come out of my chest, and I have to cross my hands together because they are about to go crazy shaking. This whole talk is getting way too close to the feelings talk, and the thought alone makes me want to jump out of my skin.

"Oh, I have no doubt that you can take care of yourself, gorgeous," he says, turning and grabbing things to toss into the pan. "But it's also okay to let someone else take care of you." I get up from the stool, my mouth suddenly dry. Walking over to the cabinet and grabbing a glass, I go to the fridge and fill it with water. "Like, for example, I want to cook you dinner."

"I'm happy to eat your dinner," I say, trying to lighten the talk and get off the track of where I think this is going.

"I want to take you out," he shares and the back of my neck starts to burn.

"I'll be sporting a baby bump soon." I smile at him. "There is no need to take me out and stake your claim."

He looks over at me for a second before turning his face back forward, moving the pot on the stove top. "I want to be by your side the whole way. All day, every day."

"You know that I'm never getting married, right?" The words come out even before I can stop them. "I mean, it's no surprise to anyone. This isn't new."

"Oh, trust me; everyone and their mother knows that you are never getting married." He laughs and I can tell that this conversation is getting him tense. I can tell by the way his hand is clenched onto the handle of the pot. "But why?"

"You're kidding, right?" I try to make a joke of this whole conversation.

"I'm not kidding," he says, walking over to grab another pot. "I've heard you say you are never getting married." I watch him walk over to the sink and fill the pot with water. "But you've never told me why." He puts the pot that is full of water on the stove and turns on the burner.

"Well, where do I start," I say and he walks over to the island where he grabs the shrimp. "Let's start with my brother."

"You mean your brother who is married to the love of his life." He turns his back to throw the shrimp in the pan. "And has two children."

I glare at him now. "Did you forget about him breaking Harlow's heart and then getting engaged to someone else?" I ask him, my eyebrows going up. "Let's not forget that detail."

"No one is forgetting that detail, but at the end of the day he's married and happy," he reminds me, and I have never hated him being a lawyer more in my life than right now.

"Okay, then move on to the shit show that happened to my sisters." I counter his objection or whatever it was. My mouth is getting dry and my neck is starting to burn.

"You mean your sisters who are happily married?" he asks me and all I can do is glare at him, that and to tell him to fuck off.

But instead, I try to keep calm. "They are happily married now." My voice goes up a touch. "But they didn't start out happily married."

He shrugs his shoulders. "They just weren't with the right one."

"Exactly my point." I throw my hands up. "They thought they were and then what?" I look at him. "Oh, no counter, Mr. Lawyer." He chuckles. "I tell you what, then they got kicked in the vagina and then up the ass getting their heart broken." I shake my head. "Nope, not going to happen. Not interested." Just the thought makes me start to hyperventilate.

"But if they didn't get their asses kicked, then they wouldn't have found out," he says and I hold up my hand.

"I know what you are going to say. They were not with the right person. Blah blah blah." He irritates me even more by laughing just a bit; okay, fine, it irritates me a lot and I ignore the fact that it's bothering me because in a way he's right. "But they still got their hearts broken. Fuck, they were going to walk down the aisle and promise forever with someone." I slap the island in front of me. "And then what."

"But they didn't," he says calmly.

"No, they didn't, they just got their hearts broken," I tell him. "I'm not going to ever put myself through that." I shake my head. "I've seen enough weddings to last me a lifetime and you know which ones I remember the most?" He just stares at me. "The ones where they get their heart stomped on. The ones where one is left sobbing and the other is just gone. I'm just not interested in it."

"Who says you are going to get your heart broken?" he asks me and now turns to look straight at me. "You can be different from your sisters and from all those other stories. You keep looking at the one that failed, even though your sisters' marriages are intact and still strong." He points at me. "I mean, Luke and Clarabella still have fucking naked Sunday. You should look at all the ones that actually took place and they are happy. Have you ever done the percentage?"

"No, because I don't need to." I have never been more adamant about something in my whole life. I just can't do it. Fuck, even watching my mother mourn my father was so hard for me to watch. I have never told anyone about what that did to me. I will never tell anyone. Listening to her cry at night for him. Watching her try to pretend she was okay, all the while she would walk around the house and talk to him. "I won't even think of putting myself in that position," I tell him, my heart speeding up and the sense of my chest being crushed. "To be that dependent on someone. Ever. So it's not even a discussion."

"Well, what about us?" he asks me and in the last twelve years he has never ever pushed me to call what we have anything. I mean, sure, we've never said we were not seeing other people while he was away and I was here. I mean, I know that I wasn't seeing anyone and I never asked him if he was seeing anyone else. Mainly because even if he said he was, I wasn't going to give him what he wanted. I never asked and he never told me. But the last six months that he's been back, it's been evident that we were only seeing each other.

"What about us?" I ask him, trying to be confused by his question. "It's me and it's you and now there is a baby."

"Our baby." He points at him and then to me. "I don't want to argue with you," he says softly. "I just want you to know that you can't get rid of me."

I roll my eyes. "I never said I wanted to get rid of you." The thought of not being with him hurts my heart, but I also know that eventually I'm not going to be with him. I've been preparing my heart for this for a while now. I just didn't think it would be so soon.

"No, but you also never said you wanted me either," he says and his tone sounds like he's hurt. "I mean, I know you like spending time with me. At least at night." He smirks and I can't tell if he's hurt or not. "I don't want to take your independence from you," he murmurs softly. "The last thing I want is for you to do something you don't want to do and then blame me for stopping you from doing it." I don't say anything or interrupt him, instead I listen to him. "What I'm saying is that I want to be there for you and the baby not because I have to, but because I want to. I want to go to the doctor with you. I want to cook you dinner or breakfast." He winks at me and I can feel that he's changing the subject. "I want to go for a walk with you down the street. I want to, I don't know, at least be able to hold your hand when I want to." He shrugs. "But to be honest, it doesn't matter what I want because at the end of the day I want you happy." I swallow the lump in my throat because all I want to say is that he makes me happy. That being with him makes me happy. I want to tell him that but I don't, I don't say anything. "Now go and watch television so I can finish cooking."

"For the record," I say, pushing away from the counter. "You make me happy," I admit and his eyes light up a bit. "And it smells delicious."

"Good." He nods at me. "Now come give me a kiss."

"So needy," I joke, walking to him and standing beside him, wrapping my arms around his waist. "It smells really, really good," I say softly and look up at him. He leans down and kisses my lips and just like the first time, everything inside me wakes up. "Now go relax and get off your feet." He motions with his head, bending down again, and rubbing his nose against mine. "Then we can go to bed and you can sneak out on me in the morning."

I can't help but throw my head back and laugh. "Funny, funny guy," I tease, turning around and walking over to the couch. I try to focus on the show that is playing on the television, but instead I place my hand on my stomach. All I can do is watch the man in the kitchen, the man who is quite literally the man of anyone's dream. Even mine if I would give myself a chance at it.

Ten

Bennett

I roll over, reaching out to grab Presley to pull her next to me. My arm finds the bed empty and I open my eyes, seeing that the side of the bed is in fact empty. "Gorgeous," I call for her, pushing up on my elbow. I look around the room, seeing that her stuff is nowhere to be found. I listen for any noise anywhere. Maybe she just got up and is in the bathroom getting dressed, but there is no noise anywhere except for my breathing. "That woman," I huff, pissed at myself for not hearing her sneak out. But in my defense, we were up at five when she wiggled her ass over my cock. It took less than thirty seconds for me to slide into her. I lie back down on my pillow, turning and grabbing my phone from the side table. Pressing the side button, I see that it's just a little after seven thirty. I swipe up, opening the phone app, clicking on recent and finding her at the top of the list.

I tap her name and then the little phone icon, putting it on speakerphone on the pillow beside me and close my eyes. It rings three times before she answers. "Hello," she groans out and my eyes shoot open as soon as I hear her voice.

"Gorgeous," I say, my heart starting to speed up as I grab the phone. "What's wrong?"

"I think the shrimp didn't agree with me." Her voice comes out as she huffs out, "I have to let," she says, and then I hear the phone drop to the floor. "Oh my God" is the last thing I hear before she throws up.

I throw the phone to the side and fly out of bed. Running to the walk-in closet and grabbing a pair of boxers and basketball shorts. Pulling a white T-shirt off one of the hangers and rushing down the steps while trying to put it on; only to run back up the stairs to get my phone that I forgot. "Fuck," I mumble to myself. I grab a baseball hat from the front closet, while I slide my feet into my sneakers from last night and my car keys on the way out. I put the hat backward as I jog to the car getting in. I connect the Bluetooth, while putting my seat belt on. Starting the car I press the voice button. "Call Travis," I say and look at the clock, seeing if maybe it's too early to call, but by the time I think this, it's already two rings in and he's answering the phone.

"What do I owe the privilege of having you call me this fine morning?" he says and I can hear Charlotte in the background calling Mama.

"Oh, good, you're up," I huff as I make my way down the street. "I was afraid I would wake you."

Travis laughs out. "It's eight," he says. "It's almost lunchtime for us." I look over at the center console seeing his name and not even understanding what he means.

"I have no idea what that means," I say, my finger tapping the steering wheel.

"I have a child who is almost one; she gets up at the ass crack of dawn," he says. "You'll know when it's your turn."

"Who is on the phone?" I hear Harlow ask him.

"Bennett thought he was waking us up." He laughs and I hear him put me on speakerphone.

"I wish," Harlow says. "The question is, why are you up?"

"I need help," I say. "Presley is throwing up and I think she has food poisoning or something like that."

"She doesn't have food poisoning," Harlow shares. "It's called morning sickness."

"Okay, let's call it morning sickness." I turn and head toward the supermarket, making a mental note to search morning sickness. "What should I do?"

"Run," Travis deadpans, without skipping a beat and I hear Harlow smack his arm. "Ouch."

"She needs to eat saltines and ginger stuff," Harlow says, her voice coming close to the phone. "Anything ginger settles the stomach."

"Okay." I pull into the parking lot of the grocery store. "So ginger ale, ginger tea, gingersnaps."

"How sick is she?" Harlow asks me, worry in her voice.

"I have no idea," I answer honestly. "I called her and she told me that the shrimp didn't agree with her and then hung up on me to go vomit."

"She doesn't know you are going to see her?" Travis asks as I disconnect the phone and get out of the car. I put the phone to my ear as I walk into the grocery store and grab a hand cart.

"What kind of question is that?" I ask Travis as I walk through the produce toward the aisles.

"Listen, I think that you should go over there," Travis says. "But knowing Presley, she's going to kick you in the balls in the middle of throwing up."

"No, she isn't." I laugh and think he might be wrong but it is what it is. I grab two boxes of saltines before rushing over to get some gingersnaps.

"No, she isn't." Harlow takes my side. "She likes him enough to have sex with him."

"Eww," Travis says. "That's my sister and I'm trying very hard not to think of her doing anything with him."

I laugh now. "We are having a child together."

"Don't remind me," Travis replies. "I'm not over the fact that you broke bro code."

"What?" I ask him, chuckling as I make my way through the grocery store.

"You slept with my sister," he says and I hear Harlow laugh. "How would you like it if I slept with your sister?"

"I don't have a sister," I remind him.

He doesn't have time to answer me because Harlow

kicks in her two cents. "Why would you sleep with his sister? Do you want to sleep with someone else?"

"As your attorney, I'm going to advise you not to answer that," I say. "But now that you answered my question, I'm going to let you go."

"Stay away from my sister," he growls into the phone and I hang up laughing. I don't even know what I'm throwing into the hand cart but it weighs a ton. I thank the Lord that I have Apple Pay on my phone because in my rush to get out of the house, I forgot my fucking wallet.

I get into the car, putting the three white grocery bags on the seat beside me, the whole time my stomach is in knots thinking about her sick and alone. When I pull up to her house, I call her to let her know that I'm here but she doesn't pick up the phone. I shake my head, walking up the step to her front door. I think about ringing the bell, but if she's in bed, I don't want her getting up, so I put in the code to the door. I turn the knob of the front door and push open the door. The house is still in darkness. "Gorgeous," I say softly as I walk through the house to the kitchen. The house has a little bit more lighting in the kitchen thanks to the big windows and the drapes that are open. I put the bags on the counter and then turn to see that she isn't on the couch. "Gorgeous," I say again softly as I make my way toward her bedroom. The room is still in darkness thanks to her curtains. I walk into her room seeing her in the middle of the bed, the throw pillows are tossed at the edge of the bed on top of her furry blanket. "Hey," I say softly and she opens her eyes. "I'm sorry, I didn't mean to wake you."

"What are you doing here?" she asks me as I sit down on her king-size bed.

"You didn't think I wouldn't come." I lean down and kiss her cheek. "I called Travis."

"Congratulations," she says, sighing and bringing the covers to her neck tighter.

"Harlow thinks you have morning sickness and not food poisoning." My hand comes up to rub her cheek.

"Harlow isn't a doctor." She looks at me, and she looks so pale. "I mean, she's a doctor but for animals."

I laugh at her. "Okay, well, just in case, I bought you some things," I say softly. "How is your stomach now?"

"There is a war going on in there." She turns on her back. "And I don't know who is winning and who is losing but either way they both want me miserable." I bend to kiss her lips softly.

"I'm sorry," I say to her. "I didn't hear you leave." I look into her eyes. "If I would have heard you sneaking out."

"I didn't sneak out." She avoids my eyes as she looks at the doorway. "I got up and left." I raise my eyebrows. "Quietly as to not wake you."

I can't help but laugh at her. "Okay, well, you need to stop doing that," I scold. "What if you got sick while driving?"

"Then that would have been a me problem and not a you problem." She folds her arms over her chest. "I'm fine," she says, and as soon as the words leave her mouth, she pushes away from me and jumps out of bed. "Don't come in here," she warns, slamming the door behind her and then I hear her getting sick. I hang my head, the need to rush in there bigger than me, but I know that if I do that, she is really going to kick me out.

"How are you doing in there?" I ask after a minute of not hearing anything. The toilet flushes and I hear the water from the sink turn on.

"Peachy keen," she mumbles and I hear her rinse her mouth out. It takes a minute more before she comes back out of the bathroom. She's wearing one of my T-shirts I left here that fits her like a dress.

She walks back to the bed, sliding in. "I brought you ginger ale and ginger tea," I tell her softly and get up. "I'm going to go and get you some with some saltines."

"Fine," she huffs and turns on her side. "I could do some ginger ale." I nod at her, knowing this is her way of accepting the help. Which makes me know that she really doesn't feel well. If she would be in tip-top shape, she would have told me to fuck off and she's fine.

"I'll go get you some." I kiss her forehead and walk out of the room. I open some of the blinds getting some more light in, after I start the kettle. I prepare a tray for her with a plate of saltines and gingersnaps. I also bring her ginger ale with ice and without ice and I make her a ginger tea.

When I walk back into the room, she is sitting up with her head on the pillow. The minute she feels me in the room, she opens her eyes. "Oh my goodness," she says when I place the tray on the bed in the middle of us. Her hand goes straight for the ginger ale with ice. "This looks so good," she says, grabbing it and bringing it to her lips. "I just got suddenly really hot." She takes one of her legs out of the covers.

"How are you feeling now?" I ask her, trying not to freak out that she's sick and maybe she should go to the hospital.

"Fine," she huffs and opens her eyes to look at me. I glare at her. "Fine, my stomach is going like this." She picks up her hand and does the wave with it. I get up and walk into her bathroom turning on the cold water in the sink and turning to grab a hand towel. I wet it and squeeze it out, returning to her bedside. The ginger ale has been finished and she has her head back and her eyes closed.

"Here." I hold out the rag to her. "Why don't you put this on the back of your neck?"

"I don't know how that is going to help," she replies, grabbing the rag from me but she puts it on the back of her neck. "But if it will get you off my back." I can't help but laugh as I walk around the bed and kick off my shoes. "What are you doing?"

"I'm going to sit by your side until you feel better." I sit down on the bed beside her with my back to the headboard. I grab the remote control, turning on the television. "You didn't think I'd leave you." I can't help but shake my head and laugh at the same time. "Why don't you rest your eyes, gorgeous." I turn to look at her but find her glaring at me, and I can't help but lean in and kiss her lips. "And save your energy instead of fighting with me."

Eleven

Presley

"Here we go. From what I read on the internet, the best thing to curb the nausea is bone broth," Bennett says, walking into the room as I walk back out of the bathroom.

"Where the hell did you get bone broth?" I ask him, dragging my ass back to bed and sliding under the covers. Today has not been a good day; it has in fact been the worst day of my life and I would not recommend it to anyone.

"I called Luke," he says to me as if that's a normal thing. "Explained the situation."

"And what situation is that?" I try not to laugh at him.

"Um," he says, holding the tray in his hand. "The one

where you ate bad shrimp." He winks at me. "And not the fact that it's morning sickness because you are with child."

"Smart move, Bennett." I smile at him. The whole afternoon he has been here, no matter how much I told him he didn't need to be here; he was just here. "Smart move."

"I aim to please," he tells me, smiling and I roll my eyes. "Do you feel better now that you took a shower?"

"And stopped throwing up." I fold my legs in front of me as he lays the tray down and I look at the yellow-colored broth. I turn my head right away and grab my phone dialing Luke, who answers right away. "What is in bone broth?"

"Oh, God." Bennett grabs the tray off me and turns to walk out of the room.

"It's bones," he answers me and I roll my eyes. "It's like knuckles, joints, oxtails, shanks, short ribs." I put my hand in front of my mouth.

"Never bring that shit into my house again," I say to him and he laughs.

"I didn't bring anything, your man ordered it." Luke can't help but laugh. "I also brought you a burger, so maybe go with that." I hear yelling in the background. "I have to let you go; it's naked Sunday and I have to get out of my clothes." I throw my phone down and get out of bed, walking down to the kitchen.

"Do you know what's in that?" I point at the soup and Bennett just shakes his head. He stands there looking like a college kid instead of a serious lawyer and I can't help but love this look also. "There is like knuckles and joints." I put my hand to my stomach. "I think for tonight I should have maybe chicken broth, or I don't know, the saltines helped."

"Whatever you want, gorgeous," he says, pouring the soup down the sink. "Do you want a grilled cheese?" I want to say no, but when he turns and looks at me, all I can do is smile. "Go lie back down," he says, walking over to the stove. "I'll be done in five minutes."

I walk back into the bedroom and get into bed. I lie down and close my eyes, just to rest them for a minute, and the next thing I know I'm blinking them awake and I'm in Bennett's arms. My head in his neck and I can't help but breathe him in. I look to see if any light is coming in from the kitchen but all I see is darkness. I think about getting up and moving away from him but he just pulls me in closer. "Go to sleep, Presley," he mumbles and for the first time I go back to sleep.

"Good morning." I feel a kiss on my neck. "I have to head out to work," he says, "but I didn't want to sneak out and make you worry about me." I stretch, laughing at his comment. "See you later." He kisses my lips. "There is water, ginger ale, and ginger tea on the bedside table."

I open my eyes and see him still there looking over me. "Bye," I say, pushing him away. "Go, I'll be fine."

"You'll call me?" he asks me, walking backward toward the door and for the first time I don't want him to go. I want him to stay, it's also the first time I slept the whole night without one foot out the door.

"No," I tell him as he turns and walks out of the

bedroom laughing.

"See you tonight, gorgeous" is the last thing he says before walking out the door and slamming the door behind him.

"Or not," I say, grabbing the ginger tea from the tray beside my bed. I take a sip of the tea and walk over to the walk-in closet, grabbing a nice white skirt with green and light pink leaves with a button-up sleeveless white cotton shirt. The strappy nude heels complete the outfit, and when I walk into the office forty-five minutes later, I'm met with a huge straw basket that sits on the table in my office.

I walk over and look inside seeing all the stuff that I have at home. "Morning." Clarabella sticks her head in. "Your man just dropped that off and told me to make sure that you are okay."

"I don't have a man," I inform her. "I can take care of myself."

"Sure you can." She laughs and I ignore her. I also ignore the fact that during the day the only thing that makes me feel better are the saltines and the ginger tea. Luckily, I have no appointments for the day and Shelby works from home and Clarabella took off at lunch. I'm about to call it a day when my phone rings and I see it's Bennett.

"Hello," I answer before I can even think about it.

"Gorgeous, you didn't text me," he huffs and his voice goes soft. "How are you feeling?"

"Great," I say, lying a bit. I did get queasy before.

"Good, when are you leaving work?" he asks me and

I can hear that he's doing something.

"Now." I get up, grabbing my keys and purse.

"Perfect timing," he says. "Stop by my place on the way home."

"I don't know what the hell is wrong with me but I had this sudden need to nap," I tell him. "So I was going to go home and get into bed."

"You have to eat," he reminds me. "So you might as well just come here and then you can nap."

"Will you leave me alone?" I huff, getting into my car. "I'll be there in ten."

"See you soon, gorgeous," he says, disconnecting.

When I park my car, I'm pissed that I came here instead of just going home. I walk up the steps and I'm about to knock on the door when it's swung open and he stands there in his dress pants and his baby-blue button-up shirt rolled up at the sleeves. "Hey, gorgeous." He wraps his arms around my waist and pulls me in for a kiss. His musky cologne always does me in. "You look amazing." I don't have time to say anything else because he bends his head and kisses my lips. My tongue comes out and slides into his mouth and I swear his kisses leave me breathless. "I could get used to this," he says, kissing my neck. "But you have to eat." He grabs my hand and pulls me into the kitchen and I'm shocked.

"What is all this?" I ask of the take-out trays that fill the whole island.

"I didn't know how you would be feeling tonight," he says, standing behind me with his hands on my hips. "So I went ahead and had all of your favorite food prepared."

I look over at everything that I love from blueberry muffins to maple-glazed salmon. "Oh my God," I say, shaking my head and looking over my shoulder at him. His black hair looks like he was nervously running his hand through it, his brown eyes look like home. I turn in his arms and wrap my arms around his neck. "I'm not saying that I'm not hungry." I kiss under his chin, loving his five o'clock shadow. "But I think I'm hungry for something else." I nip under his jaw. "Something meatier." I lick his jaw as my body tingles with anticipation. His hands grip my hips harder than before. "Something that is more of a muscle." Sex with Bennett is never fucking dull and I have to say neither of us hold back when it comes to this. If I want something, I have no problem telling him, just like if he wants me to suck his cock or ride him, he will come right out and say it. I can't tell you the number of times we would be on the couch and all I would have to say is *I'm horny* and we'd be naked and his head would be buried between my legs.

I kiss his neck and turn to hold his hand, bringing him over to the U-shaped couch. "Gorgeous," he says and I look over my shoulder and my chest tightens. He's been my dream man since I can remember. "You really need to eat," he says to me, but instead I push him down onto one of the ends. He opens his legs and I step between them, his hands roaming up the back of my legs all the way up to my bare ass, while he looks up at me. "Unbutton my skirt," I tell him as I run my hands through his hair. The skirt falls to the floor, puddling around my feet. "Lie back." I push him back and he lies down. I crawl onto the couch with him, my knees on the sides of his hips.

My pussy sitting right over his covered cock, I move my hips side to side. Falling forward on one hand, my face rests right on top of his. "Gorgeous," he hisses as my lips fall on his, his tongue coming out to slide into my mouth. His hands move to my sides, slowly moving to the front of my white shirt. He moves his head to the other side while his hands unbutton my white shirt. Our tongues play with each other as he finally gets all the buttons undone. Then I feel his fingers moving to my back and in a split second my bra is snapped off. I sit up on his cock now, suddenly wishing I took his pants off before I started this. He slips the shirt off my arms and the bra falls forward and is thrown across the room. "Fuck." His hands cup my tits and my nipples are so sensitive ever since I found out I was pregnant. I could come just from him playing with them. My hips move up and down on his cock and my whole body feels like it's on fire.

I move out of his reach and rub my hand up and down his covered shaft. "We should have gotten these pants off before." I lick my lips as I unbuckle his belt. He's already kicking off his shoes. I don't even wait for his pants to be off him before I bend and lick the top of his cock. The salty taste of his precum hits my tongue right away. "Hmm," I groan, taking his cock into my mouth. His nice, thick, hard cock, just the feeling of him in my mouth and I'm wet. I wrap my hand around his shaft while he pushes my hair away from my face. His hand grips my hair in his fist, and when I look up, he's watching me suck his cock.

"That's it," he says breathlessly. "Fuck." His eyes never leave mine. I lick up the shaft and twirl my tongue around the head of his cock. "How wet are you?" he asks me and I don't answer him. Instead, I slide the hand that is jerking his cock and move it to my pussy. Moving my thong to the side I slide two fingers inside me. My eyes close from my own touch, and I fuck myself with my fingers a couple of times.

"This is how wet I am," I tell him, holding up the fingers that were just inside me. His hand grabs my wrist and he yanks my fingers to his mouth as he sucks them clean. I take his cock back into my mouth. "So what do you think?" I ask him between sucking his cock and jerking it off. "Am I wet?" I lick all the way down to his balls.

He growls at me when I take one of his balls into my mouth, sucking softly. "You're about to get a lot wetter."

Twelve

Bennett

I watch her suck my cock and it's the hottest thing. I'm totally lying; every single time with her is hot. She gives just as good as she gets, it's always been like that. This is the one place that she lets all her guards down. I growl at her when she sucks one of my balls into her mouth, my mouth tasting the sweetness off her fingers. "You're about to get a lot wetter." I sit up, surprising her as she gets on her knees. My hand goes to the nape of her neck where I grab a fistful of her hair and pull her mouth to me. Our mouths feast on each other, she sucks my tongue exactly how she sucked my cock.

My hands grab her hips and I flip her around, so she's on her back and I'm between her legs. She opens for me and pulls her knees up knowing that in a second my mouth is going to be on her. Removing her thong I see that her pussy glistens in the light, and before I bend down to lick her, I use my middle finger to rub up and down her slit, slipping inside her. "Always wet for me." Her eyes close as I finger-fuck her with one finger, her hands cupping her tits as she tweaks her nipples.

"Yes" is the only thing she pants out as I move my finger out of her and to her clit. My finger going around and around in soft circles.

"Tell me what you want?" I ask her and her eyes open to stare at me. Her blue eyes are light, but the more I rub her clit, the darker they become.

"I want you to suck my clit and finger-fuck me," she says, not skipping a beat, "until I come on your hand." I move my hand down and slip two fingers inside her. "Yes, like that." She moves her hips up a bit to get my fingers into her faster. "And then after I come," she pants, "I want you to sit on the couch and I want to slide my pussy down your cock." My cock twitches at her words. "While you hold my hips and help me ride you."

"Fuck," I say, bending my head, my mouth going to her clit and sucking. Her pussy clenches around my fingers and I know that she's getting close.

"After I ride you for a couple of minutes"—my eyes look up and find her watching me—"I want you to lay me on my back and fuck me harder than you've fucked me before." Her legs close in around my head. "Then I want you to flip me over and fuck me from behind." I fuck her pussy faster with my finger. "Make my ass red."

She moans out the last words before she comes all over my fingers, drenching them. "Bennett," she chants my name over and over again, thrashing her head side to side as one orgasm rolls into another. "I need your cock," she says as her legs fall to the sides of her.

"Your wish is my command." I slip my fingers out of her and lick them clean while she watches. I unbutton my shirt, pulling it off me and tossing it in the pile of clothes beside us.

"Sit," she commands me as she gets on her knees. I sit down with my back to the couch while she throws a leg over my hips, squatting over my cock. I can't help but lean in and take one of her nipples into my mouth. Sucking it in deep and then biting it at the end. Her head goes back and she moans for a second before she reaches down in the middle of her legs and she grabs my cock in her hand. She rubs it up and down her slit before positioning it at her entrance as she moves her hand, and inch by inch she slides down my cock until I'm balls deep in her. "So full." She leans forward to slip her tongue in my mouth. Her forehead is on mine, her hands on my stomach as I hold her hips in my hands and help her ride me. She lets go of my lips for a second and we stare into each other's eyes as she slowly fucks me. Our panting fills the room, her wetness all over my cock; only the last couple of days we've gone without condoms because it was a little bit too late. "Bennett," she pants my name as my hands go from her hips to squeeze her ass, moving up her sides, and coming up to grab both tits in my hands. "It's so good," she praises and she sits up straight and moves up and down, this time faster than before.

"What is it, gorgeous?" I ask her as she leans back. "Your pussy is getting tighter." I lick my thumb and find her clit for a second before wrapping my arms around her waist and turning her on her back. "Play time is over," I tell her and she smiles at me.

"Is that a fact?" I slide into her pussy, slamming the last inch in. "You going to fuck me hard?" she asks me as I pull out slowly and then just slam into her. The sounds of our skin slapping together fill the room. "Is that all you have?" Her eyes almost roll to the back of her head as I slam into her again. Over and over again, I pound her pussy harder than I ever have before. "Give it to me, Bennett."

"You have it," I tell her as I feel her pussy clench down on me, her juices running down my balls. "You have all of me," I mumble right before slamming into her one more time and this time coming in her.

"I feel you," she says as I plant myself all the way inside her, "coming in me." I put my forehead on hers. "Your cock gets bigger inside me." She slips her tongue in my mouth as I collapse on the side of her.

"Are you okay?" I ask her from her side as I try to catch my breath.

"I'm more than okay." She beams and I turn to the side and she hitches her leg over my hip, my cock still planted inside her, still hard. My hips move slowly fucking her. "If you are going to fuck me again." She moves her hips to me. "I'm going to need to eat." My hand comes up to cup her tit, rolling her nipple. "Or we can eat later," she says and I fuck her again just like she wanted me to.

"I DON'T THINK I can eat another bite," Presley says from her stool beside me. I look over at her, and she is wearing my button-down shirt with nothing under it. I sit on my own stool in just my boxers, that I had to put on after the third round. We not only had two rounds on the couch, but when we came into the kitchen, she bent over right in front of me and I couldn't help myself.

"Well, you sure worked up an appetite." I lean over and kiss her neck and then her lips.

"I wasn't the only one." She raises her hand and holds my cheek.

"I have an idea," I say, pulling her stool even closer to me.

"The last time you had an idea." She laughs and I can't help the fullness that I feel in my chest. "You 'accidentally' put it in the wrong hole." She uses her fingers to put accidentally in quotations.

I can't help but laugh. "It was an accident," I tell her, getting up and walking toward the stairs. "Stay there," I urge her and she rolls her eyes at me. I jog up the stairs and walk into my bedroom, going straight for the bathroom.

I turn on the lights walking across the white marble floor with gray in it and turn on the water in the giant tub. Adding some of the bubble bath that I know she likes, I put a towel on the floor to make sure that she doesn't slip when she comes out. I walk over to the double-sink vanity that is in front of the tub, grabbing the candles from under the cabinet. Lighting the candles, I walk over to the doorway and dim the lights, giving it a soft glow. I walk back over to the tub and adjust the water, knowing she likes it warmer. I walk over to the shower and grab her loofah, tossing it into the water. "What are you doing?" she asks me, standing in the doorway.

"I said stay there." I stand and she walks into the bathroom to stand in front of me. "Why don't you listen?"

"Since when have I ever listened to you?" She laughs as she looks over at the tub filling with water.

"I wanted to surprise you," I tell her, wrapping my arms around her and pulling her to me. She gets on her tippy-toes to kiss me and wraps her arms around my shoulders. "I was getting the bath for you."

"What?" she says, surprised.

"I wanted you to relax." I kiss her lips and then go to her cheek. My arms drop from her as I unbutton the two buttons that were keeping my shirt on her. "I got this," I say and turn my head. "Play spa music." The sound of soft crashing waves fills the room now. "Get in," I invite her, holding out my hand so she can get in the tub.

She shakes her head and puts one foot in and sighs before moving her other foot in. She pulls me to her. "Aren't you going to get in with me?" she asks me and there isn't anything I wouldn't give this woman.

"If that's what you want," I say, letting her hands go and taking my boxers off and tossing them with my white shirt that she took off. I get into the tub and sit down, opening my legs for her to sit between them. I'm expecting her to sit facing me but she doesn't; instead, she sits down with her back against my chest.

"This is so nice," she says, putting her head to the side. "It's just what I needed and didn't know."

"Did you have a long day?" I ask her, grabbing the loofah and washing her arm.

"It wasn't that bad," she says, turning and kissing my arm. "I called the doctor."

I stop moving, putting the loofah down. "And?"

"She gave me an appointment for Friday," she tells me and I kiss the top of her head. "See, I do listen to you sometimes."

I can't help but laugh at that statement. "In the last twelve years you've listened to me a total of maybe twice.

"Did you tell your mother?" I ask her and she chuckles.

"Did she show up at your office?" she counters and I laugh now.

"She would show up, wouldn't she? She's going to show up and probably hand me my ass on a platter."

She laughs as I wrap my arms around her, holding her stomach. It feels like I'm holding my whole world. "Do you want a girl or a boy?" I ask her softly, my thumbs moving up and down.

"I didn't really think about it," she answers me softly. "You?"

"As long as the baby is healthy, I don't care if it's a boy or a girl." I can't help the smile that comes to me now. "As long as they have your smile."

She turns to smile at me. "I want them to be smart like you." I don't make the correction that she said them, meaning we are going to have more than one child together.

"I want them to have your eyes." I kiss her temple. "And your hair."

"I want them to be loyal like you." She looks up at me and I'm about to tell her that I want them to never go a day without knowing they are loved but instead I just lean down and kiss her lips, silently telling her that I'll love her always.

Thirteen

Presley

"I'm running out." I walk into Clarabella's office. She is sitting at the table that faces outside. She is on her iPad uploading pictures of the food she took this weekend to the website. "I have an appointment at one."

"Appointment?" She looks over at me. "What appointment?"

"It's private," I say to her and she shakes her head.

"Shelby!" she yells for my other sister and I roll my eyes. I knew that I should have just told them I was going to work from home.

"You rang," Shelby replies as she walks into the office and heads straight for the couch.

"Presley has an appointment." Clarabella leans back

in the chair and Shelby's head probably has whiplash the way she looks over at me.

"What appointment?" she asks me with worry in her voice.

"It's nothing," I say, folding my arms over my chest. "I have to go in and meet my OGBYN." I try to keep my voice stable. They both gasp out. "And this is why I didn't say anything to you guys."

"Oh my goodness," Shelby says, putting her hand to her chest. "I can't wait."

"No." I point at her. "No one is coming with me."

"You're not going to the appointment alone," Clarabella tells me.

"I'm not going alone," I mumble and then quickly want to walk out of the room.

"Ohhhh," Shelby teases, clapping her hands. "Are you going with your baby daddy?"

"That's going to be his new nickname." Clarabella smiles at me and I walk over to one of the chairs next to her and sit down. "I'm going to change it in my phone right now."

"Can you not call him that," I say, shaking my head, not adding that he's more than just my baby daddy, he's also probably one of my best friends. And if things were different, I stop the thought right away. "And can we just like, not, you know"—I wave my hands—"go crazy."

"I spoke to Mom this morning," Shelby says and I glare at her. "Relax. I didn't tell her you are with child."

"Yeah, what is up with that?" Clarabella asks.

"Nothing is up with that, it's just I want to speak to the

doctor before I say anything to anyone." I tap the table with my finger. "Imagine telling Mom and then finding out it's a false alarm."

"Five pregnancy tests are not a false alarm." Shelby laughs. "I mean, one maybe, but five."

"Even if I tell her, she's going to ask me all these questions and I'm not going to know any answers, so I'm going to go to the doctor and then go and see her."

Shelby picks up her phone. "What are you doing?" I hiss at her but can't say anything else before Mom picks up the phone.

"Hey, Mom, it's me," Shelby says. "I'm really craving some home cooking."

"Is that so?" my mother says, and you can tell from her tone she doesn't believe her. "Then go home and cook."

I can't help but laugh quietly and flip her the bird. "Presley called a family meeting," Shelby informs her and I glare at her. "And I figured you would want to be included. But," she sings, "it's fine. I'll fill you in on the details later."

"What do you mean a family meeting?" my mother says. "Presley," she calls my name knowing that I'll be in the room.

"It's nothing, Mom," I say while I mouth the words "I fucking hate you" to Shelby. "I'll come over after work."

"Why can't you girls leave me in peace?" my mother shrieks out. "Why do you all do this to me? My blood pressure is already through the roof."

"Can we be a little bit more dramatic?" Clarabella

says, rolling her eyes.

"Don't you even start," my mother snaps at her. "Mrs. Rutherferd said she was walking down the street the other day and caught you and Luke on the front porch going at it hot and heavy." Shelby and I both whip our heads to her.

"It was dark outside," Clarabella says. "And no one saw anything; we were under a blanket."

"In the front yard!" my mother shouts. "You have a whole house to do that in." I can just picture her hands going crazy in the air.

"We started outside and finished inside," Clarabella clarifies for her. "It's like we were dry humping, it's fine." She smirks. "We kept it PG-18."

"I'll see you all at six," my mother says, disconnecting, not even continuing this conversation.

"You're welcome," Clarabella says and I laugh. "She's so distraught about me, you having a baby out of wedlock might be the least of her worries."

"You are insane," Shelby declares. "Her having a baby out of wedlock will push her to cover all the mirrors in her house and mourn."

"She's going to walk down Main Street with a veil over her head and sit in the park feeding pigeons," Clarabella cuts in. "Like the girl from *Home Alone 2*."

"Oh, God, you are both ridiculous." I get up. "I'll call you when I'm done."

I walk out of the meeting and walk into my office when I hear the front door open. I'm grabbing my purse when I hear my name being called over the speaker.

"Presley, your baby daddy is here." Clarabella giggles. "And he's looking dapper AF."

I groan and walk out of my office, seeing him standing in front of Clarabella laughing. He's wearing a black suit that molds to him, with a light gray button-down shirt. His hands are in his pockets and it makes his arms even bigger. "What are you doing here?" I ask, walking to him.

"I figured that we can go to the doctor together," he says to me. "And then maybe go for lunch."

"Is that code for go and put more baby batter in you?" Clarabella says, laughing.

"You are so gross," I retort, turning and walking out of the office, ignoring the fact that I'm so nervous I feel like I'm going to vomit. I walk over to his car and feel him right behind me. "I really wish that you would have told me you were coming here today."

"Well, if you didn't sneak out of my house this morning," he says, opening the door for me, "I would have told you."

"Oh, now it's my fault." I get into the car. "If you think of kissing me right now, I'm going to…"

"I would never kiss you out in public," he says sarcastically, "and have people think we actually like each other." I roll my eyes. "We are having a baby together, people are going to know we've kissed."

"I don't want to be late," I state and he just nods his head, shutting the car door and walking around the car.

He gets in and neither of us says anything to each other after I give him the address. His phone beeps about fifty times on the way to the doctor. "Someone is a social butterfly," I tease when he parks as he grabs his phone.

"I'm in the middle of a merger," he tells me, looking down at his phone. "I'll turn it off."

I reach for the handle of the door and push it open, stepping out. Every single step feels like this overwhelming dread coming to me. I've been nervous and anxious for the last two days and I'm ignoring all the screaming that is going on in my head.

We walk into the waiting room and I give my name to the secretary, who smiles at me and tells me to come on back. Bennett puts his hand on my lower back as we walk into one of the examining rooms. "The doctor will be right in," she says. "If you can undress the bottoms." She hands me one of those blue big paper sheets.

I look over at Bennett, who is reading one of the posters on the wall that shows the baby in different stages. "We should get one of these," he says as I slip off the skirt I'm wearing, "and put it in my office at home."

"Or we don't and just look it up online," I suggest, wrapping the blue sheet around me and it doesn't even fit. I walk over to the examine table and sit down. The sound of crinkling has Bennett looking over at me.

"Are you okay?" he asks me. I roll my eyes only because my heart is beating so fast in my chest that I'm afraid if I say something, anything, it'll come out with a tremor.

His phone beeps and I just glare at him. "Sorry, I thought I turned it off," he says, taking the phone out of his pocket but looking at it for a second.

"You don't have to be here." The words come out of my mouth and his head whips around to me. "I mean, if you're busy, it's fine. I can get an Uber."

He doesn't have a chance to answer me, and maybe it's a good thing, because I'm afraid that at this rate I don't know what else is going to come out of my mouth with all these nerves. "Hi there." A woman comes in. "My name is Cynthia and I'm the nurse." I smile at her as she walks over to the desk and moves the mouse, which makes the computer screen open. She goes over my name and age. "When was your last menstrual cycle?"

"Six weeks ago," I say, my legs now moving with the nerves in me. I look over at Bennett, who stands there trying to read the screen to make sure that she's putting everything in right. His hair is perfectly set today and he looks so handsome. The nurse gets up and walks out. I look over at Bennett and I'm about to tell him that I'm not feeling myself but I don't have a chance because the door opens again.

"Presley," the other woman says, coming in. "I'm Dr. Wellington." She smiles and then looks over at Bennett. "You must be daddy."

I can't help the smile that comes on my face looking at Bennett's face light up. "That would be me," he says, standing by my side now and putting a hand on my back. She sits exactly where the nurse did, reading the notes in the chart. "It says your last menstrual cycle was six weeks ago."

"Yes," I tell her as she turns the lights off in the room. "If you will lie back and put your feet up, we will get the show on the road." I nod at her, lying back until my back hits the table. I put my feet in each stirrup, my stomach lurching now. " Since you are under eight weeks," Dr. Wellington says, "we are going to go in with the wand." She rolls over to the middle of my legs grabbing the white piece from the machine beside her.

"Is that going to hurt the baby?" Bennett says, stepping forward holding out his hand.

"The baby will not feel anything," she calmly tells him while she rolls a condom down on this white wand. "I'm going to insert this in and you will see the baby, hopefully," she says, putting lubricant on the wand. "It might be too early to hear the heartbeat but we can see the heart beating on the screen." Bennett stands beside me and puts his hand in mine. "This might be cold," she says, and I squeeze Bennett's hand when she sticks the wand inside me.

"It's okay, gorgeous," he says softly, rubbing my head with his hand.

"There he or she is," the doctor says and we look over at the monitor. "I'm just going to check a few things," she informs us as she clicks away on the machine.

"Is everything okay?" I ask, my heart speeding up and the tears pouring out of my eyes as I look over at what is my baby.

"Yeah, everything looks okay," she says, taking the wand out of me. "I'm going to check you out this way," she explains, grabbing a white bottle, pushing the blue paper down, and squirting gel on my lower stomach. She grabs another thing and puts it on the gel. "Okay, so this is your baby's heartbeat," she says and the sound of galloping fills the air. I can't stop the tears that come to me, even if I tried to fight them off. I look over at Bennett, who just stares at the screen, his own tears running down his face. "I'll take a couple of pictures," she states and she snaps and presses some buttons. She wipes off my stomach and then the machine, going over to turn on the lights. "Okay, well, everything looks good," she confirms and then looks down, and I can sense that she is holding something back. "But from my calculations, you are just starting your eleventh week."

I open my mouth and look over at Bennett, who just stares at her with his own mouth open. "No, I think there is a mistake. I had my period."

"That is normal," she tells me. "It's not abnormal to get your period the first couple of months. Were they heavy?"

"Um, I know that one month was more spotting than a full-blown period and it lasted a couple of days." I look at her and she smiles.

"Well, that could have been a clue," she says and I can feel the back of my neck burn.

"But I just got morning sickness," I inform her, knowing that she must be mistaken.

She shrugs. "The human body is our biggest mystery." She laughs. "Regardless, you are almost done with your first trimester." She gets up now. "Congratulations." She hands Bennett the pictures that she took. "I'll see you in a month." She walks out of the room and the only thing that is going through my head is the fact that I'm almost three months along.

"We are going to need to get a second opinion," I whisper, getting up. "She obviously has no idea what she's doing." I put the blue sheet on the changing table as I get into my thong and skirt. "Almost eleven weeks," I mumble to myself, shocked, and look up to see Bennett still looking down at the pictures in his hand.

All he can do is look at me as he smiles from ear to ear. "I need to get a frame."

Fourteen

Presley

"Look at the feet." Bennett turns the picture for me to see but my head is still spinning. "I don't know"—he looks back at the picture—"it might be a girl."

"Bennett," I say between clenched teeth. "This can't be," I try to whisper-yell at him. "She's wrong. We need to get a second opinion."

"What?" he says, shocked, and holds the pictures to his chest. "We were right there, we saw the screen."

"Well, her screen is broken." I put my shoes on, huffing, "She said I was eleven weeks, and that's impossible."

"No, it's not." He shakes his head. "She said it's normal."

I put my hands on my head. "You know what isn't

normal," I tell him. "Me being almost twelve weeks and not even showing." All I can think to myself is, how did this happen? My head is still spinning at this news.

"Your boobs are bigger." He points out and I glare at him. "What? You don't think your boobs are bigger?"

"They are not," I say, but just this morning I noticed that they are fuller. "More sensitive, yes."

He shakes his head. "Nah, they're fuller now." He holds up his hands like claws. I roll my lips, about to tell him to fuck off when there is a knock on the door.

"Yes," I say out loud and the door opens and the nurse sticks her head in.

"Is everything okay in here?" she asks.

I smile at her and say, "Yes," at the same time that Bennett replies, "No."

"We are fine," I say with a fake smile and then turn to Bennett. "Aren't we?"

"No," he says, shaking his head, "my girlfriend…"

"Not girlfriend," I correct him and now it's his turn to glare at me.

"The woman with the child in her"—he points at me—"that is mine." He points at himself and everything in me wants to stab him right now. "Is not comfortable with some of the details that the doctor told her. Would there be any way where we could get a second opinion?"

The nurse looks at him and then looks at me. "Of course," she says. "What is making you uncomfortable?"

"It's not that I'm uncomfortable," I start to say, getting flustered. "It's just that she said I was close to eleven weeks. And well, I've had my period."

"I can get the ultrasound technician to come in and give you another opinion," she says, smiling at me. "Let me see if I can get her."

All I can do is smile at her until the door is closed and then turn to glare at Bennett. "What is wrong with you?" I ask him and he looks at me with a confused look on his face. "Why would you tell her I'm uncomfortable?"

"Because you are." His voice is very calm as he walks over to me putting the pictures down on the table. He holds his hands up to cup my face. "Hey," he soothes and my hands shake as I look at him. "This is going to ease your mind, so why not just ask?" He kisses my lips softly. "It's okay to ask questions." I don't have much time to think about anything or say anything to him because there is a knock on the door. "Trust me," he says and I just roll my eyes.

"I trusted you to put the condom on properly, and look at what happened there," I mumble as the door opens and a woman comes in.

"Hi," she says, smiling at us. "I was told that mommy has questions for me."

Bennett's hands fall from my face and he puts one around my shoulder. "Yes," I finally say. "The doctor threw me off with the dates and said I was eleven weeks. And, well, I only missed one period."

"I can understand how that would be confusing," she says, putting her hand in her lab coat. "If you want, I can check it again just to put your mind at ease." I nod at her. "But having a period while pregnant in the first trimester isn't that irregular. It happens to thirty percent of women." She walks over to the computer and opens up the ultrasound report. "This is an ultrasound of a six-week scan." The picture looks like a blob if I'm honest. "And this is yours."

"Oh, well," I say, seeing that it actually looks like a baby.

"If you want, I can take measurements just to confirm it, but these tell me what your doctor said was correct."

"But will the bleeding harm the baby?" Bennett asks her for me.

"If you start bleeding now at this stage"—she looks at me—"it's more concerning than last month. This period that you had, was it heavy or just spotting?"

"I can't really remember, but I know that the last one was like spotting for two days." I think back. "It was a busy time that month, so I chalked it up to stress."

She smiles. "Well, the good news is that your first trimester is almost over."

"Thank you," I say to her, "for answering my questions."

"Don't be shy," she tells me. "Your body is going to be changing in the next six months and we are here to help you in any way we can. Trust me, there is no question that is stupid or that we haven't heard before." I don't say anything to her; instead, I just nod at her and she turns to walk out of the room.

"There, are you happy now?" Bennett says, grabbing the pictures that he put down.

"No," I lie to him, "but now I have to go and tell my mother."

"Do you want me to come with you?" he asks me and I just shake my head.

"No, I think I should do this alone," I reply to him and he nods at me and follows me out of the room.

I make an appointment for the next month and he puts it in his phone. "Is there any way to cut this?" he asks the receptionist, handing her the picture of the two sonograms. She grabs a pair of scissors and hands us back the two pictures. "Here, so you can show your mom."

"Thank you," I say softly and look down at the picture, my heart speeding up for a second before I put it away in my purse. The drive to my mother's is quiet, and when we pull up, he just looks over at me. "You sure you don't want me to come in and take the focus off you?"

"I'm having her grandchild." I laugh. "There is nothing, and I mean nothing, that is going to take the focus off me."

"This is true," he says. "Will you call me later?"

"No," I say, getting out of the car, "I might be held hostage." After I close the door, he rolls the window down and I can hear him laughing.

"Godspeed, gorgeous," he encouragess and I just shake my head walking up the driveway. I hear him drive away and my stomach sinks.

I take my phone out and call Clarabella, who answers right away. "Hey."

"I'm at Mom's," I tell her and then hear the front door open and she walks out with the phone at her ear.

"You don't say," she says with Shelby right behind her. "You think we didn't know you would come right here."

"I wasn't missing this for anything in the world," Shelby declares. "If I had to camp here for the week, I was willing to do that."

"We might as well get this over with," I say, walking up the steps and putting my phone away. "I'm going to need you two to take a shot of scotch for me since I can't."

"So we are with child?" Clarabella asks me and I glare at her. "I can see that this child is taking away all the fun in you." She turns on her heels. "Mom, your baby is home."

I look over at Shelby. "It's going to be fine."

"Lies," I mumble, walking into the house and finding my mother standing in the living room with tears already running down her face. "Why is she crying?"

"She thinks you're dying," Clarabella states.

"I wish," I say under my breath, looking at Shelby who is pouring two shots of scotch. Clarabella joins her and they click the glasses together before downing the shots.

"What is wrong with you two?" my mother shouts, throwing her hands in the air. "Your sister"—she looks back to me—"has news."

"I do have news," I confirm, walking into the living room and deciding that perhaps I should sit down for this. I let out a deep breath. "I don't think there is any good way to say what I'm going to say."

"Like a Band-Aid," Shelby says, coming to sit next to me.

"Oh, God," my mother utters, sitting down on the lone chair looking at me. "How bad is it?"

"I'm pregnant." I say the two words, never taking my eyes off my mother. There really is no other way to come out and say it. The minute I say the words, my hand goes straight to my stomach holding it, almost as if I'm protecting the baby from something.

"What?" Clarabella says, shocked. "This is brand-new information." She comes over and sits on the other side of me.

"Shut up." My mother glares at her and then turns her glare to me. "What do you mean, you're pregnant?"

"I mean, I think it's pretty much self-explanatory," Shelby says, trying not to laugh.

"I'm eleven weeks pregnant," I share, and now even my sisters gasp out.

"That's like three months," Clarabella says.

"I know," I say, opening my purse and taking out the picture, my baby. I stare down at the picture of my child and I can't see through my blurry vision because of the tears filling my eyes. My baby is the only thing that comes to my mind; the tightness in my chest makes it feel like my heart is coming up to my throat. "I was just as shocked. I even needed to get a second opinion, I was that much in shock."

Shelby grabs the picture from me and just beams. "Aww," she coos, handing it over to Clarabella.

"Presley Marie Baker," my mother grinds out with clenched teeth as she gets up, "you better tell me what the fuck is going on."

"She swore," Clarabella whispers. "This does not bode well, don't look at her. Look away." She looks down at her hands.

"I don't think she needs to draw you a picture, Mom." Shelby laughs, leaning back on the couch.

"You"—my mother points at her—"mind your business. You"—she points at Clarabella—"not a word." Clarabella pretends to zip her mouth and throw away the key. "You"—she points at me—"talk."

"Well, like Shelby said, I don't think there is much to say." My mouth goes suddenly dry. "According to the doctor, everything is fine."

"Who got you pregnant?" she asks me, sitting back down.

"Say Jesus," Clarabella says under her breath, pretending to look around her.

"I don't know if that matters," I avoid, getting up wanting to walk to the bar and take a shot, but instead I walk over to the kitchen. The whole time all I can hear is my heartbeat echoing in my ears. The nerves take over and fill my body and my hand shakes as I pull open the fridge. The back of my neck gets hot and even my armpits start to get a touch sweaty. I'm about to grab a bottle of water but then see sweet tea beside it and choose that instead.

"What are you talking about, it doesn't matter?" My mother gets up and turns to look at me.

"I mean, it doesn't matter," I repeat, pouring myself some of the sweet tea and drinking it. "This would be so much better if it was peach flavor."

"She's worried about peach tea when she should be worried about who the father is." My mother throws up her hands.

"Relax there, Mom." Clarabella gets up. "She knows exactly who the father is." I glare at Clarabella. "What? You don't think she's going to find out when he's, I don't know, in the delivery room with you?"

"Ugh, fine," I concede but then look at my mother. "You can't freak out," I say, knowing that she is going to freak out and knowing that her freaking out isn't going to help the fact that inside I'm freaking out just as much.

"Why would I freak out?" My mother puts her hands on her hips. "When have I ever freaked out?"

Shelby holds her hand up to say something and one look from my mother stops her. "Never"—she shakes her head—"you've always been calm, cool, and collected." Shelby then looks at me. "And go."

I think about maybe not saying his name, but I know he already told Travis, and I know that eventually it's going to come out. "Fine"—I brace myself—"the father is Bennett."

My mother looks at me in shock, her mouth opening. "This is brand-new information," Shelby says and Clarabella just laughs at her.

"Bennett," my mother says. "Bennett, Bennett?"

"I mean, I don't know how many Bennetts you know," I say, "but yes." The smile fills my face when I say his name and think about how happy he was to have the baby's picture.

She gasps out laughing, clapping her hands together.

"This is wonderful news. I mean, so…" She looks at me and we are all shocked that she didn't freak the fuck out. And only when she says the last sentence do I know why. "When is the wedding?"

Fifteen

Bennett

*P*ulling into the parking lot, I wonder if maybe I should have called before coming. But as I look around, I don't see that many cars. I get out of the car and walk up the steps to the building, grabbing the handle and pushing the door open.

The bell rings above the door at the same time that I hear what sounds like fifty dogs start barking. "Oh, my," I say, looking around to see if any of them are coming my way.

One of the back doors opens and I look over when I hear footsteps. Around the corner comes the receptionist. "Oh, hey, Bennett." Petra smiles at me. "What brings you here?" She's been the receptionist here for a couple of years.

"I was wondering if Travis is free?" I put my hands in my pockets.

"Let me see." She turns around, going to the back, while I turn and look at the pictures that are on the wall. All different families with their pets, one family with a pet pig. I laugh thinking that I should bring this up to Presley and see if she wants to get a pet together.

"You can go on back," Petra says to me, and I nod walking down the hallway that she just came out of. "It's the last door on the right." She walks over to her desk to pick up the phone that started to ring.

"Thank you," I reply, making my way to the door and turning the handle, stepping into the room. The minute I walk in, I know that I should have called before coming. "What the fuck are you doing?" I look at him as he looks down at the dog in front of him on the big silver table. He is lying down on his side with a tube in his mouth. Travis is dressed in scrubs with plastic glasses on his face and a surgeon cap atop his head.

"I'm neutering the dog," he says, as if it's nothing and my hand goes directly to my penis as if I'm shielding my own balls.

He chuckles as he tugs on, I don't even know what. "What the fuck?" I hiss. "Why would you tell me to come back here if you were doing this?" I look down at the dog. "Should this be a private moment?"

"You came to see me," he says, not paying attention to me. "It's not that big of a deal. I come see you at work all the time," he reasons as he plops down what I can see looks like a testicle. I put a hand to my mouth thinking I'm going to be sick.

"I'm a lawyer!" I shriek. "What do you see when you come in my office? Manila folders."

"Oh, come on," he says, tugging on something, "it's not that bad." I shake my head. "Anyway, what do I owe the pleasure of your company this fine afternoon?"

"Well, it's official," I say, smiling at him and taking the picture out of my pocket. "We are having a baby."

"Aww," Travis says, smiling at me, "I'd come and give you a hug." He holds up his arms and his gloves are covered in a bit of blood.

"I'm good, thanks." I hold up my hand and look down and see the picture again. "She's eleven weeks."

Travis whistles and looks at me with big eyes. "That's almost past the danger stage."

"Danger stage?" I ask him, my heartbeat speeding up with the word danger. I mean, it can't be good with that word.

"It's past the twelve-week mark," he explains to me. "Chances to miscarry happen before the twelve-week mark."

I open my mouth. "Why would they not tell you that?" I ask him, wondering if maybe Presley should stay in bed for the next week, just to keep things inside.

"They try not to scare you." Travis shrugs. "It's fine; you should get one of those baby books."

"What baby book?" I tilt my head to the side and almost kick myself. Why didn't I look this up online?

"I have one in my office I'll give to you," Travis says

and smiles at me. "How is Presley taking all this?"

"Um." I hesitate, trying to think of the words. "Well, she wanted a second opinion."

Travis throws his head back and lets out the biggest laugh I've ever heard. "Of course she did ."

"I think she was in shock, finding out she was further along than she thought she was." I smirk. "These change everything." I hold up the paper.

"It sure fucking does." Travis looks at me.

"I thought you should also know that she's in the middle of telling your mother about it right now." His eyes almost bug out of his head.

"Fuck, I wanted to be there for that," he hisses. "My mother is going to lose her shit."

"She's going to be fine."

"I really hope Clarabella tapes it," Travis says. "Maybe we can catch some of the screaming on the Ring cam that I installed."

"There will be no screaming." I try to convince myself of that, but knowing Mrs. Baker, there will be screaming, there will be crying, and hopefully she doesn't come over to my house with the frying pan she used to threaten us with when we were younger. "She's going to be fine." I smirk at him. "Besides, after what the three of you did to her with your weddings, this is going to be a walk in the park."

"Oh, you poor son of a bitch." Travis shakes his head and looks down at the dog, doing I don't even know what now. "You think that it's going to be easy." He chuckles. "What are you going to do?"

"I'm going to ask her to move in with me," I inform him, and Travis's eyes go big. "Officially."

"Is there an unofficial way to ask someone to move in with you?" he jokes with me.

"She sneaks out of my house every single time she's there." For the first time ever, I say it out loud, "And I'm tired of it." My voice trails off and I look down at the picture of the baby, our baby. "I want her and the baby to be with me always."

"I mean, she can't sneak out of your house with a baby." Travis points at me. "I don't know what she is going to say, to be honest." He shakes his head. "What if she says no?"

It's my turn to laugh. "I can be persuasive." He just stares at me and I get knots in my stomach. "Stop looking at me like that and pay attention to the dog that just lost their family jewels."

"Well, whatever you need from me." He grabs the needle next to him. "Just let me know." He starts to stitch up the dog.

"I'm going to go home and cook her favorite meal," I say, starting to formulate a plan.

"Didn't you cook for her a couple of days ago and she threw up?" My mouth opens as I look at him. "Nothing is sacred."

"Apparently not," I huff. "Okay, I have to go and maybe pick up some flowers and woo the shit out of her." Just saying the words out loud I feel like I'm going to throw up. "I'm going to get out of here"—I point at the door—"and leave you with…" I point at the dog.

"Buster." Travis fills me in on the dog's name.

"Buster"—I lean down—"it's going to be all right." Travis just laughs.

"Call me later and tell me how it went," Travis tells me when I turn and grab the handle of the door. "I'll say a prayer for you."

"I know that your sister likes me at least." I look over my shoulder at him and he just smirks. "A little."

"I meant for my mother," he retorts, and I flip him the bird before walking out of the room. When I walk down the hallway, Petra is on the phone, so I just hold up my hand and walk out.

Getting into the car, I stop first at the grocery store, where I pick up all the ingredients for chicken fried steak, looking down at my phone every two seconds to make sure I grab the right things. "I should just call Luke," I mumble as I make my way through the aisles, and when I walk out of the store, I'm holding seven bags full of stuff. "This better fucking work," I tell myself after I close the trunk and get back into the car, going straight for the flower shop.

The minute I step inside, the scent of flowers hits my nose. Every single way I turn, there are different flowers. "How may I help you?" the lady asks, coming out from the back room.

"I'm thinking I need some roses, maybe?" I scratch my neck. "Peonies are her favorite flowers," I inform the lady, who doesn't need to know any of this.

"We just got some fresh peonies"—she points to the right—"in a variety of colors." She walks over to the five big plastic bins.

"Do peonies scream *move in with me*?" I ask, looking over at her and she just laughs at me. "I was thinking more like roses," I tell her. "Roses everywhere and then some rose petals sprinkled on the floor."

"That could work also." She walks over to what looks like a field of roses. Rows and rows of roses in all different colors.

"Is there a particular color that goes with *move in with me*?" I ask her, taking out my phone and getting ready to google it.

"Oh, honey, if you are this nervous about asking her to move in with you"—she laughs at me—"can you imagine when it's time to get down on one knee?"

"Oh, I would do that also," I tell her, "but figured I'd ease into it."

"That sounds like a great idea." She smiles at me. "How about you get some peonies since it's her favorite?" She points back to the peonies. "And then some roses to sprinkle throughout the house."

"That sounds even better than my plan." I snap my fingers. "So I'll take all the peonies." I turn back to the lady whose mouth is now hanging open. "And then let's go for about, what do you think, a hundred roses?"

The lady chuckles at me. "If she doesn't move in with you." She winks at me. "I might."

I can't help but laugh because the lady has to be in her early sixties. "Well, I'll keep your number just in case," I joke with her.

She throws her head back and laughs even more

now. "It'll take me a couple of minutes to get everything together," she explains and I just nod at her.

I pull out my phone, bringing up Presley's name.

Me: How did it go?

I press send and wait to see if the three little dots come up. When they don't, I send her another text.

Me: Just left Travis's office and I'm going to head home. I have a surprise for you.

I press send and scroll my emails while I wait for her to answer. The lady comes back out with one bouquet wrapped in brown paper. "Now you are going to need to make several trips," she says, and it takes me about thirty minutes to get all the flowers in the car.

The nerves set in as soon as I get home, and instead of texting her, I call her and it goes straight to voice mail. "Gorgeous," I say after the beep, "I'm getting worried, call me." I press end, making my way into the house.

My hands are literally shaking with nerves and my stomach rolls every single time I think about her. I pick up my phone again when I'm about to start cooking and text her.

Me: Where are you?

I put the phone down, thinking she might be at home and sick, the thought has me running out the front door and rushing over to her house. The sun has set now, and when I pull up to her house there are no lights on and her car isn't in the driveway. *"What the fuck?"* I think to myself. Picking up the phone and calling her again, hearing her voice mail click on. "Gorgeous," I say softly, "you need to call me."

Sixteen

Presley

"You call me tomorrow," my mother says when she hugs me goodbye. "And we can talk about things." She puts her hands on my arms, smiling at me.

I look over at Clarabella, who literally rolls her lips. "Mom, there is nothing to talk about. I'm not getting married." It's the same thing I've been telling her for the past three freaking hours. The minute I told her that I wasn't getting married, she threw her hands in the air and pretended to faint on the chair. But then she shot right back up and started pacing back and forth, having a conversation with herself. My sisters and I tried to interrupt her, but all we heard was, "Why me? Why can't it just be easy for one?" If we tried to talk to her, she would glare at us.

"Presley, honey." She tries to use her soft voice, but I can tell she's one second away from shrieking. "Think of the baby." Her eyes roam down to my stomach.

I laugh. "I am thinking of the baby." I put my hand to my stomach. "She or he will be raised by two parents who love them. And then they have you."

"But," she says, and she quickly stops talking.

"Mom," Clarabella says. "Why don't we just take that she is giving you a grandchild as a win?" I hold up one hand to Clarabella, telling my mother to listen to her. "I mean, just last month she was a lone wolf with a house full of cats."

I roll my eyes. "I wasn't with a house full of cats," I defend, annoyed. "It was a couple." I stop talking when I feel the phone vibrate in my pocket, but if I take it out, my mother is going to want to know if it's Bennett, and it probably is. Then she is going to want him to come over, and well, today has been crazy enough as it is. "Now, I'll be a lone wolf with a cub."

"Why can't one of you just…" My mother throws up her hands, and there is the woman who we all know and love. "Do things the easy way?"

"She's having a child out of wedlock." Shelby sticks her two cents into the conversation when she comes out of the front door. "If that doesn't scream easy, I don't know what does."

I can't help but laugh at that. If only they knew that he was the only man I've ever slept with. "I shall walk around Main Street with an A on my chest," I deadpan over my shoulder, walking down the front steps. My mother gasps at even the thought.

"Idiot," Clarabella says. "The A stands for adultery." She laughs. "We can cross that off your résumé."

"It's still early," Shelby replies, kissing my mother and following us down the steps.

"Which one of you is driving the pregnant lady home?" I ask my sisters.

"I will," Clarabella volunteers. "It's on my way to pick up Luke."

"Perfect," I say, walking over to Clarabella's car. She unlocks the door, and I get in, grabbing my phone right away. Looking down, I see that I have a couple of missed calls from Bennett and a couple of messages. I smile when I see that he has a surprise for me, and when Clarabella gets in the car, I almost tell her to drop me off at Bennett's house.

"You okay?" Clarabella asks when she pulls away from my mother's house.

"I mean, no one died." I try to make a joke out of it. "And I didn't throw up."

"At one point"—Clarabella laughs—"I thought Mom's head was going to explode."

"That would have been too easy for anyone." I look out the window. "How long do you think it's going to take her before she corners Bennett and tells him to put a ring on it?"

Clarabella laughs. "Two days max." I can't help but think she's right. "And she's going to use the *you want to buy the cow if you are going to drink the milk*."

I can't help but throw my head back and laugh. "Oh, she's definitely going to use that." I stop talking when a sharp pain runs through my stomach, and I yell out.

"What the fuck?" Clarabella asks, and I look over at her.

"I just had," I start to say when another pain hits my stomach. "Sharp pain," I say, panting now.

"Maybe you have to poop," she says when she pulls into my driveway. I get out of the car and rush up the stairs when I feel it.

"No," I say, shaking my head. "No." I throw everything on the floor and head straight into the bathroom. Not even bothering to close the door, I look down and see the blood in my underwear. "Oh my God," I say, sitting down. "Don't panic," I tell myself, looking up and seeing Clarabella standing there now. Her face is white like a ghost. "Spotting is normal." I don't know if I'm telling her or convincing myself. I wipe myself, and it's not spotting. It's bright red blood. "That is not spotting."

My whole body just shuts down, and I feel this whole sense of dread come over me. "We should go to the hospital." All I can do is look up at Clarabella, not sure what to say or do. "Come on," she urges softly, picking me up off the toilet bowl and pulling up my panties my skirt falls down over my legs. "Let's get going." She puts her arm in mine as she walks me down the hallway, only stopping to pick up my purse and phone at the front door.

I don't even know how I make it to the car. Everything inside me stops. My body feels like it's on the outside looking in. She gets in the car, and I look over at her.

"Don't tell anyone," I say softly as she nods her head, reversing out of my driveway. My heart rises to my throat.

I close my eyes, not sure I can stand to look at her as she drives. My hand rests on my stomach the whole time as I hold the baby in the palms of my hands. *This isn't happening* is the only thing I can repeat over and over to myself. When the car comes to a stop, I open my eyes and see that we are in the parking lot of the emergency room at the hospital. "I've got your purse," Clarabella says, and all I can do is nod at her. The lump in my throat is so big, if I say a word, all that is going to come out is a sob.

The doors slide open as soon as we get close to them, walking into the white room. There are brown chairs everywhere, and most are empty. "Hi," Clarabella greets when she stops, and I look at her talking to a lady sitting behind a glass partition. "My sister is eleven weeks pregnant, and she got a sharp pain in her stomach, and now she is bleeding."

The lady behind the glass looks at her and then at me. "I need her insurance papers, please." I move my eyes from her. She asks questions, and Clarabella answers them all. "Someone will call you shortly."

"But I'm bleeding," I say, my voice trembling, looking at her, and she gives me a sad look.

"I'll see what I can do." She gets up, and I look over at Clarabella, who tries not to show me that she's worried, but you can see she has this fear in her eyes.

"It's going to be fine," she comforts, smiling and trying

to calm me down. I turn to walk to the brown chair, but we don't have time to sit down before my name is called.

I feel like I'm in a trance, my feet are moving because they need to. We walk through another brown door, and this time, there is a nurse there waiting. "Presley Baker?" I don't know if she is asking or telling, and the only thing I can do is nod my head. "Right this way." She turns, and I follow her, not realizing the whole time that I'm holding my stomach.

"The doctor will be right in," she states when she puts us in a room. "Just sit on the table." She points at the same table I was in this afternoon. But it's different. Everything about this is different. So fucking different.

"Do you want me to call Bennett?" Clarabella asks, and my head snaps up as I look at her.

"No," I say. My heart beats so fast in my chest as I sit on the table. The back of my neck burns with nerves. When the door opens, a man walks in wearing a white coat.

"Presley Baker." He says my name, looking down at the white paper in front of him.

"Yes," I say, my voice trembling. "That's me."

"Okay, it says here you are eleven weeks and started bleeding," he says, reading whatever is on the paper.

"Yes," I confirm, and Clarabella comes over to stand beside me. I don't even feel the tears running down my face until they drop on my hands that are holding my stomach.

"And you are eleven weeks?" he asks, and I just nod my head. "There is not much we can do." He looks at me. "If you are miscarrying the baby, there is nothing we can do to stop it."

Miscarriage. The word makes me close my eyes. "How?" Clarabella asks for me. "She was fine this morning." It's almost as if she can read my mind, and she is my voice. Right now, all I want to do is close my eyes and wake up from this nightmare.

The doctor says something, but instead, I just close my eyes. All I can do is picture Bennett in my head holding the picture of the baby in his hand, wearing the biggest smile I've ever seen. He's going to hate me. The thought runs straight to my head. He's going to hate me for not taking care of the baby. If anything happens to the baby, it's my fault. I raise my hand to wipe away the tears. "I had an ultrasound this afternoon." I interrupt whatever it is they are saying. "And it was perfect."

"We can check for you now again," the doctor says. "At least we can see if your baby still has a heartbeat." I look over at Clarabella, who puts her hand to her mouth at the same time that the phone rings from my purse.

"Turn it off," I tell her, and her eyes fly to mine. The thought of facing him is too much for me to bear right now. Today when he looked at the picture of our baby, I had never seen him smile as big as he did, and now it might be over. "Turn it off."

Seventeen

Bennett

"What the fuck is going on?" I hiss to the empty room and toss my phone on the couch next to me. I'm sitting on the couch in my living room in the dark. After driving from Presley's mother's house, I made my way back to Presley's house, thinking maybe I missed her on her way home. But when I pulled up and walked up the steps to ring the doorbell, I found all the lights off. I punched in the code on the door and walked in as I called her name. I took the steps two at a time and found her bedroom in darkness. There was no sign of her in the house. I slammed the front door behind me as I got back in the car and went to her office. *Maybe she went there to grab her car,* I tell myself, trying to keep the bad thoughts at bay. "Pick up, pick up, pick up." I willed her every single time I called her, but all I got was her voice mail.

My heart calmed down when I pulled into the parking lot and saw her car still there. She was probably working since she took some time off this afternoon. But it was only for a moment. When I ran up the steps to the front door, it was locked. I walked around to the back like a creeping Peeping Tom, only to find that everything inside was closed and dark. I went back to my house, hoping maybe she was there waiting for me, but all I came home to was a house that smelled like a field of flowers.

I put my head back, rubbing my face with both my hands, the knots in my stomach getting bigger and bigger as the seconds feel like hours. "Where are you, Presley?" I ask the empty room, hoping that maybe by saying her name, she will magically appear. I get not answering my calls when she was with her mother, but I know she's not there, and something in me tells me something is wrong. Or it could be my head playing tricks with me. Either way I'm about to get desperate enough to call her mother, and that isn't going to be good for anyone. I think about calling Travis, but what am I going to say? "Your sister isn't answering my phone call." It sounds so juvenile

I grab the phone again from beside me, dialing her again, expecting it to ring four times before going to voice mail, but this time, it doesn't. The minute I hear someone say, "Hello," I sit up and my heart speeds up again.

"Presley?" I say her name even though I know it's

not her. She probably lost her phone, which is why she hasn't been calling me.

"No, it's Clarabella." Everything in me turns cold, yet I have no reason for it. The way she is talking is very soft and feels as if she's trying not to be heard.

"Hey." I try not to sound so anxious. "Sorry I didn't recognize your voice. I was looking for Presley." I swallow the lump that has now moved from my stomach to the middle of my chest, and now it's stuck in my throat. "Is she there?"

"Yes," she says, and I hear rustling on her end. "But she can't come to the phone right now."

I'm about to say what the actual fuck out loud, but instead, I reel it back in, but not as good as I had it planned in my head. "Okay," I snap. "What the fuck is going on?" I close my eyes, ready to kick myself for how that came out.

"She's," she whispers softly and then I hear the sound of her heels clicking on the floor. "She's with the doctor." The hairs on my neck stand up when she says those words.

If I thought I was ready for whatever she was going to tell me, I was wrong. My feet are moving even before I realize what is going on. I'm out the door and in the car. "Where are you?" So many things are going through my head, but none of them good. All of them bad and all of them lead me to be without one of them, and I can't even fathom that thought. The thought alone feels like razor blades cutting into my flesh.

"She's going to kill me," Clarabella huffs, and I can

hear her voice tremble, and my heart breaks. "I don't—"

"Clarabella," I cut her off. "You can either tell me where you are," I say between clenched teeth as I back out of the driveway, "or I call your mother." I know it's a low blow, but I have no choice. "And then spend the rest of the time calling every single hospital until I find her."

"Wow," Clarabella says. "I'm at Memorial." She names the hospital, and I don't even know if I say goodbye. All I know is that I hang up. I rush over there, and the whole time my head is screaming that she didn't call me. Why didn't she call me? I shake my head, and the fear that I had before now turns into nerves. I pull up into the emergency parking lot and pull in the first open spot I find. Grabbing the keys and my phone, I don't even know if I close the door before rushing to the entrance.

I run all the way to the door, rushing in sideways as the door opens at a snail's pace. I look around the room with brown chairs everywhere, not seeing Clarabella. My eyes look everywhere to see if there are signs to direct me to maybe a maternity ward. I look down at my phone, calling Presley, but it goes straight to voice mail. I take a couple more steps into the room, and when I spot a woman sitting behind a glass window, I walk over. "Excuse me," I tell her, and she looks up from her computer. "I'm looking for Presley Baker."

"Are you family?" she asks as she turns to the computer.

I swallow before answering her. "I am not."

"We can't give out personal and confidential information to non-family members," she tells me, and I know that she is sticking to protocol, but right now, all I can think about is getting to Presley.

"They just called me from here," I lie just a bit. "I'm the father."

She looks me up and down, and it feels like she's judging me for not being here before now, and if I were here, I would probably be doing the same. "Wait here." She pushes away from the desk and gets up, going I don't even know where. I run my hands through my hair. Taking my phone out of my pocket, I call Presley, but it goes straight to voice mail this time, and I'm about to throw the fucking thing against the wall when I hear my name being called.

"Bennett." I look over and see Clarabella coming out of a hallway. Her face is streaked with tears as she pretends she is okay. I look around to see if Presley is with her, but she's alone.

"Where is she?" I ask. My mouth suddenly goes dry, so dry I can't swallow.

"She's being monitored," she shares, and I take a step toward the hallway, and I'm stopped.

"Clarabella." I say her name, almost hissing. "You can tell me where she is, or I go to jail finding out where she is. I'm at my fucking wit's end right now."

She holds up her hands. "I know," she says softly. "I'll take you to her." She turns, and I follow her, not saying another word.

As I walk down the white corridor, I scan all the rooms looking for her. My head is going around and around with all these questions, but no answers are given. When

Clarabella stops, she looks over at me. "I know you are freaking out, but go easy in there."

I just nod at her, not sure how my voice is going to come out. I'm also not prepared for what I'm walking into. I step into the room after Clarabella, seeing Presley sitting up in the hospital bed. "Hey," Presley says when she looks at me. I can see the dried tears on her face. She looks pale, and her hand is on her stomach, and I have to wonder if everything is okay.

I stop mid step looking at her. She's even wearing a hospital gown. "I would have come sooner," I tell her, still not going to her. Not sure I can.

"I'll give you two a minute," Clarabella says, looking at Presley and then giving me a sad smile on the way out.

"Why didn't you call me?" is the first thing that comes out of my mouth. The pressure on my chest feels like an elephant is sitting on it while a tiger comes by and rips my heart out.

"It was no big deal." She tries to smile but nothing comes. "I was spotting a bit, so I came here to make sure that I was okay." My stomach that was in my throat has now sunk to my feet.

"You were spotting a little bit." Not sure I understand what is happening. "You were bleeding."

"Yes," she answers and wipes the tear off her cheek. "But the baby is fine." She answers the question I've been dying to know. "The doctor came in and checked me before and we heard the baby's heartbeat." She puts her hands on her stomach. "He's going to monitor me for a couple of hours." She shrugs, trying to pretend that it's nothing. "So like I said, it was no big deal."

"It wasn't a big deal," I repeat her words, my voice

staying monotone. The picture of her coming here scared out of her mind flashes before my eyes. The other picture that flashes before my eyes is me not being here with her. The thought is almost too much to bear. I should step out of the room and calm myself before we talk about anything else.

"Yes, there wasn't a reason for us both to freak out." She avoids looking at me and looks down at her stomach.

"I thought we were doing this together." When my voice comes out almost broken, her eyes fly up to mine as she looks at me in shock. Her eyes look into mine, and I don't think I'll ever love anyone as much as I love her. I also know that she will never love me like I want her to.

"We are doing this together," she reassures me, but the only thing I can focus on is that she went through this without me.

"But then this happens, and you don't even call me." The tears fill my eyes. "You don't send me a message." I shake my head. "I drove around looking for you, worried. I had no answers. I had no idea that all this time you were here going through all of this, and I was none the wiser."

"I didn't think…" she says, and I hold up my hand to stop her from talking. The more she talks and tries to make this not a big deal, the angrier I get.

"Unless you did think and didn't care." I laugh bitterly, knowing that this moment is the moment I've been dreading. The moment that I knew would somehow come, yet didn't want it. The moment that makes my heart shatter in my chest. "I've been a fool all this time."

Eighteen

Presley

"Unless you did think and didn't care." He laughs, and I can tell it's a sarcastic laugh. My heart beats in my chest so hard and fast I feel like I'm going to throw up. My hand on my stomach grips the sheet with nerves. "I've been a fool all this time."

"Bennett." I say his name as the stinging of tears rushes to my eyes. I blink them away as fast as I can, but nothing can prepare me for what comes next. My mouth goes so dry that swallowing hurts, and all the words get stuck at the back of my throat not able to go past the lump that is there. "Everything just happened so fast," I finally am able to croak out. "The doctor came in." I don't tell him the truth. I don't tell him that I didn't want to call him because I couldn't face him if something had happened. I don't tell him that the only thing I wanted was to have him here with me. I don't tell him that even though Clarabella was here with me, the only thing I wanted was to look into his eyes.

He shakes his head, the defeat written all over his face. "I've loved you for the past twelve years." The words come out like he's in pain. "With every single fiber of my being, I love you." My lower lip trembles, and the tears now come without warning. The look of anguish is all over his face, and it hurts me to my core. "I love you, Presley." A lone tear runs down his face. "I don't know why I thought maybe, just maybe, you felt the same." His hand moves up to the back of his neck as he holds it.

"But you knew." The words come out without me thinking. "You knew that I was never going to get married." He stares into my eyes, and he looks like he's going to say something. "I never changed my mind on that."

"I didn't care if we got married. I didn't have to be married," he says. "All I wanted was you. I would have taken you any way I could have you. I would have given you whatever it is you wanted." His hand falls from his neck. "I just fucking wanted you." *You have me,* I want to yell out at the top of my lungs. *I'm yours.* But I don't even have a second to come back before he continues, "I won't burden you anymore with my feelings." Just when I thought it couldn't get worse, it does. "I won't burden you with being stuck with me, at least not romantically." The need to sob out grips my whole body, and I fight it back. *This is what you wanted*, I remind myself. "We are having a baby together, and that will be my main focus." I sit up now when he stops talking, and I'm about to tell him that I do love him, but the door swings open.

"I come bearing snacks," Clarabella says with a smile on her face, and she stops mid step when she takes in the standoff that is happening. The smile fades from her face. "I have juice also." She looks at Bennett and then looks at me. "Is everything okay?"

"Just fine," Bennett says. "I'll be in the waiting room." He doesn't even look my way before turning and walking out. I watch the door close softly behind him, my vision blurry from the tears that have built up and are now falling over my lids and down my face.

"What just happened?" Clarabella walks over to the side of my bed, putting down the snacks and juice she got on the bedside table.

"Nothing," I reply, using the back of my hand to rub off the tears from my cheeks. "I'm just worried about the baby," I say, putting my hand back on my stomach, thinking not so long ago when I found out that the baby was okay.

When the doctor walked into the room and told me that there was nothing he could do, it's almost as if I didn't hear the words. It was Clarabella who was my voice at that point. "If you don't want to do your job as a doctor, then can you send someone else in who will." He was taken aback by her tone. "And if that is the case, we can go to another hospital." I didn't want to tell her that I wasn't fucking leaving here.

The doctor nodded at her and looked back at me. "The first thing we are going to do is check and see if there is a heartbeat." He walked over to the sink to wash his hands. "Lie back, and if you can, pull your skirt down to your hips." I did what he asked me to do. "I will tell you that if you are in the process of a miscarriage, there is nothing we can do about it."

"Can we stop saying that fucking word?" Clarabella hissed. "And see what's going on in there." She pointed at my stomach, and the doctor sat down on the stool and wheeled himself over to the light and turned it off before he wheeled back to me.

I had no idea what to expect. I had no idea what I was looking at, but when he put the blue gel on my stomach and pressed the thing down on it, and I looked over at the monitor, I let out a sob when I saw my baby still there. Very much in the same position as this afternoon. He moved from right to left, and then he pressed a button, and you could hear what sounded like galloping horses. "That's the heartbeat," he said, and I just put my hands in front of my face and sobbed.

"Why is Bennett in the waiting room and not by your side?" Clarabella asks, and I grab the bottle of apple juice. I twist off the top and take a sip. The cold sweetness hits my tongue right away. "It's okay to tell him that you need him."

"No, it's not," I snap. "It's not okay." I shake my head, the tears coming again.

"Presley," she says softly. "You are having a baby with him." She puts her hand on top of mine.

"And he can be as involved as he wants to with the child." The words taste sour in my mouth. "He knows this."

"What did he tell you?" she asks, and when I look up at her, I know she has an idea.

"That he loves me." I finally say the words, and I don't add that I love him also, because what difference does it make?

"I mean, that's a good thing, right?" She smirks, trying to be the voice of reason. "There is nothing wrong with admitting that you want him," she urges softly. "It's not going to make you less of a woman if you admit you love and need him. It's okay."

"No, it's not," I say angrily. "It's not okay." I wipe my cheek off with more force than I wanted to. My hands are shaking. "It's the opposite of okay. I can never give him what he wants."

"Why not?" She sits up and folds her arms across her chest.

"Because," I huff. "That isn't the way it goes."

She rolls her eyes and laughs at me. "And how does it go?"

"Look at Travis," I start. "He was supposed to marry Jennifer, and then what?"

"Then he didn't." She shrugs. "Then he got his head out of his ass and married Harlow, just like he was always supposed to."

"Look at Shelby," I counter and don't even give her a chance to answer. "She was head over heels in love with Joseph, and he fucked her friend."

"One, he's a douchebag, so there is that." Clarabella holds up her finger. "And two, she was always supposed to marry Ace."

"What about you?" I look at her. "Were you always supposed to marry Luke?" She glares at me now. "Were you always supposed to marry Luke?"

"Yes," she says without even thinking about it. "Now that I can look back on it. Knowing one thousand percent that I was always supposed to marry Luke. Look at Bennett." Just hearing his name hurts my heart. "He's been home for the past six months, and he's been at your beck and call this whole time."

I'm about to say that he hasn't when the doctor comes in again. "Okay, Ms. Baker," he says. "Let's see how we are doing."

"Do you want me to get Bennett?" Clarabella asks, and I just nod my head. No matter what, I told him that I would never keep the baby from him. She gets up and walks out of the room.

"The father is in the waiting room." I don't even know why I'm telling him this.

"Have you gone to the bathroom?" he asks, and I shake my head. I was too afraid to go to the bathroom. "If you can, go and check and see how the bleeding is." I nod at him, turning and getting out of the bed.

I walk to the bathroom in the corner, and when I pull down my panties, I see dried blood. My heart starts to speed up when I sit down and pee. I close my eyes for a second after I pee, trying to gather the courage to wipe myself. I grab the toilet paper. "You better be clean," I say under my breath. "Also, you are very grounded when you come out for scaring me like this. But I love you." That's the last thing I say before I look down and see a clean piece of toilet paper. With not even a pink tint to it.

I walk out of the bathroom with the biggest smile on my face. "No blood," I tell the doctor as the door opens, and Clarabella comes back in with Bennett behind her.

"What happened?" Clarabella asks, and my eyes go to Bennett, hoping that he looks at me, and he does for a second. The hurt and pain are so evident it makes my whole body hurt.

"No blood," I say, walking to the bed, afraid that at any moment, my knees are going to give out on me, and I'm going to be lying in the middle of the floor.

"That's good news," the doctor says when I get back into bed. I pull up the cover to my waist as the doctor lowers the head of the bed a bit. I lift the hospital gown up but keep my private area covered with the blanket. "Let's see how the little one is doing." I look up at Clarabella, who stands beside Bennett at the foot of the bed. My eyes don't move from Bennett as he puts his hands in his pockets and looks at the monitor and then the doctor. My whole body cries out for him. My hands shake as I grab the bedsheets beside me. I plead with the universe to let him look at me, but no one is listening tonight. The sound of the heartbeat fills the room, and my eyes go from Bennett to the screen. The weight of almost losing the baby is taken off me. I put my hand in front of my mouth as I cry, but this time, they're tears of happiness. My baby is going to be okay, at least for today, and I have this sudden need to put my hand back on my stomach to protect him or her from anything. The tears quickly turn to a smile that is so big on my face it hurts my cheeks. The baby looks like it's doing somersaults in there. I look down at my stomach in awe that I feel nothing, not even a little tickle. I look back at Bennett, and his eyes are just on the screen. "You have a very active baby." I wait for Bennett to say "*We have a very active baby,*" but he doesn't. The doctor turns off the machine and wipes my stomach. "I'm going to suggest that you stay off your feet for a couple of days and rest." He turns on the lights. I don't tell him that the idea of sitting in bed and not doing anything for the next two weeks has played over and over. "I'll send a report to your doctor, and you can do a follow-up with her."

"Thank you," I tell him. "For everything."

"I'm going to wait outside," Bennett says, turning to walk out of the room, and I want to yell at him to stay, but instead, I watch him leave as my heart shatters in my chest.

Nineteen

Bennett

"I'm going to wait outside," I say before turning and walking out of the room. The whole time, my body and my head tell me to go to her. The whole time, I had to fight with my eyes not to look at her.

When I walked out of the room the first time, I took two steps down the hallway and had to stop and put my hand against the wall to help hold me up. Walking away from her has to be the hardest thing I've ever done in my whole life. Telling her I love her, knowing that it might be the end of us. Standing in that room after going crazy looking for her and finding out that our baby may be lost and her not even bothering to call me was too much. I should have taken a second to think about it. I should have just walked away and gathered my thoughts. I sat in that waiting room with my heart broken from walking away from her, yet full from learning that the baby was okay.

I don't even know how long I sat there. It was as if I was in a daze. As if the world around me was going full force in a circle like a tornado, yet I sat in the middle of it just watching the destruction and devastation around me. When Clarabella came out to get me, I thought she was going to tell me that Presley wanted me. I had this little glimmer of hope in me that she did love me, but once I got inside, she told me the doctor was there. The light from the candle of hope that I had going on was blown out.

Now I'm sitting in that chair again, my whole body feeling like it got run over by a Mack truck. Front and back. I lean forward, putting my elbows on my knees, and just hang my head. How did this day go from one of the best days of my life to the absolute worst day of my life in a blink of an eye?

I hear footsteps and turn my head to look up and see them walking toward me. Presley has her head looking down as Clarabella says something to her. When she looks up, I make the mistake of looking into her eyes, and it just shatters me again. *She doesn't want you*, my head screams, and I exhale a deep breath before getting up. "Hey," I say, looking at Clarabella, afraid to look over at Presley. "Everything okay?"

"Peachy keen," Clarabella replies.

"Okay, I'm going to head out." I point with my thumb

toward the door. "Let me know if—" I stop talking. "Just, I guess, keep me informed."

"Of course." Presley's voice comes out so soft if I wasn't paying attention, I would think I made it up. Everything in me wants to take her home and make sure she's well taken care of. I want to take her home and put her to bed. I want to take her home just to take her home, but instead, I nod my head at them and turn to walk out of the hospital.

I sit in my car and watch them come out, neither of them talking. I think about following them to make sure she gets home okay, but I don't. Instead, I make my way back to my house, walking in and the smell of flowers hits me right away.

"Fuck." I walk into the kitchen and get a huge black garbage bag. I walk around the room, taking the flowers and tossing them away. After cleaning up, I turn off the lights and walk up the stairs. The phone in my hand is almost as if it's a cement brick, getting heavier and heavier as the minutes tick by.

No matter what I do, I can't shut off my mind. Stepping into the shower, all I can see is her sitting in the hospital bed staring at me. Lying in the bed on my pillow, the only thing I can smell is her beside me. I watch the hours tick by like years, and finally, when the sun comes up, I get up and walk downstairs to make coffee. I pick up the phone for what is the millionth time since I got home to see if she texted me, but she hasn't. "I guess no news is good news."

When I walk into the office, I put my things down on

my desk and walk down the hallway to see one of the partners. Knocking on the open door, I stick my head in to see Damian. "Hey there," I say, and he looks up. "Mind if I come in?"

"Please," he says, taking his glasses off and putting them on the papers in front of him. "Come in."

"Thank you. If you have a second, I would love some advice," I tell him, and his eyebrows pinch together.

"Close the door," he says, and I nod, closing the door and then walking over to sit in one of the chairs facing him.

"This is fucking weird." I laugh nervously as Damian leans back in his chair. I can tell from the look of confusion on Damian's face that his head is spinning. "I need a lawyer," I state and then let out a huge breath that I've been holding. "Fuck, this is harder than I thought," I say, the pain hitting me in my chest.

"Take it one step at a time," he says and gets up from his chair, walking around the desk. He comes to sit next to me in the chair beside me. "Do I need to get the other partners in here?"

"No." I shake my head. "I need a family lawyer." He just looks at me. "I'm going to be a father."

"Holy shit," Damian says with a smile on his face. "Congratulations."

"Thanks," I say, smiling. "It's a great surprise."

"Are you and the mother…?" he starts to ask, and I shake my head.

"We are not." Those three words come out of my mouth, and then the lump forms. So big it feels like those boulders that you put in place to stop things from coming out. "I want to know my rights."

"What do you want realistically?" he asks.

"I want to be able to raise my child fifty-fifty." My eyes sting with tears that come. "That's all I want." My voice trails off because the only thing else I want is to be able to raise the baby with Presley by my side. But that isn't in the cards for me. "I don't know what else to ask for."

"How about I draw up a contract?" he suggests to me. "And we can go over things."

"Yes," I tell him. "And if you don't mind, I'd like to keep it confidential for now." He nods at me, and I get up. "I'll be around if you have questions."

"I'll work on this myself," he says when I get to the door, and all I can do is nod at him. I try to get lost in my work, and it only works half the time. The other half of the time, I'm sitting in my desk chair looking out the window, wondering what she's doing.

I'm sitting on the couch drinking a beer as I try to focus on a baseball game when the doorbell rings. My feet are moving before I can think about it, and the minute I open the door, all the hope that I had that it would be her is gone. "Hey." Travis stands there with a bottle of scotch in his hand. "Clarabella called and said you might need a drink." I pfft out and turn back to walk toward the kitchen. I grab two shot glasses and turn back, watching Travis sit down on one of the stools. "I'm assuming she said no."

"Didn't even get there," I tell him, holding out my

hand for him to give me the bottle. "She started bleeding." Travis gasps when I say those words. "She's fine. The baby is fine." I hold up my hand before he freaks out. "But let's just say, I wasn't her first call." He looks at me, his mouth still open. "It is what it is," I say, shrugging and not bothering to make eye contact with him. I pour two shots of scotch, handing him one.

"What are you going to do?" he asks while I down a shot and then quickly pour myself another one. The burning of the second shot is even worse than the first one.

"There isn't anything for me to do," I share. "If she needs help, I'll always be there. But my main focus now is on the baby and co-parenting in the most civil way possible," I say, taking another shot.

"I wish I knew what to say," Travis says to me as he takes his first shot.

"Nothing you can say," I tell him. "I have to accept that this is how it's going to be, and we move on." I take another shot, and this time, I hiss.

Travis sits with me, neither of us saying anything. "Call me if you need me," he says when he gets up. "Even though she's my sister." He looks at me. "You're like a brother to me." I tilt my head to the side. "Fuck, that was gross."

I can't help but chuckle a bit when he turns and walks out, slamming the door behind him. I pick up my phone and press the button to see the screen saver picture of Presley and me. My finger rubs over her face slowly, and I turn off everything, then walk upstairs to bed.

I don't even know how the week goes by. I can't even tell what day it is. But when I get the papers from Damian, I know that I have to make the phone call. I grab my phone, and the whole time, my hands shake as I press the phone icon. I put the cell phone in the middle of my desk before I press the green button next to her name. I don't even know if she is going to answer. All I can hear right now is the beating of my own heart. And then everything stops when I hear her voice. "Hello." Fuck, this is harder than I thought it would be.

"Hey," I greet nervously, almost stuttering. "It's me."

"Hi," she says softly.

"Sorry for disturbing you on a workday." My hands rest on my desk around the phone.

"You can call me at any time," she affirms, and all I can do is hang my head.

Block it out, I tell myself. Just say what you need to say and then move on. "I was hoping that we can set up a time to talk." My finger taps on the desk at the same time that my leg starts to move up and down.

"That sounds like a good idea," she says. "Should I come by your place tonight?" *No,* the right side of my head yells. "Or do you want to come over to mine?" *Yes,* the left side of my brain says.

"I was thinking that you could come by the office," I say. "No rush, whenever you have time."

"I can be there in thirty minutes," she responds. "Is that too soon?"

"No, that sounds great," I say. "See you then." I don't wait for her to say anything before I press the red button. I lean back in my chair, and I feel like my shirt is shrinking on me. I prepare myself mentally for her arrival. However, there is nothing that will ever prepare me for Presley.

I look up when I hear a knock on the door, and there she stands. She's wearing dark blue pants that go high on the waist with the same color belt and a white silk shirt tucked in. "Hi." She smiles as she walks in, and even though she's smiling, she looks like she is tired. Everything in me wants to ask her if she's sleeping. But I know I can't ask her that. She made her decision and I have to respect it.

"Hi." I get up from my chair and walk around my desk. "Thanks for coming so quickly." I try to remain calm, but my hands are wet with sweat.

"Of course," she says. "Should I close the door?"

I shake my head. "No." I grab the file on top. "Why don't we sit down in the conference room?" I say to her as I walk to her. "Do you want a water or something?"

"I'm fine," she says, and all I can do is nod at her, motioning with my head to follow me. We walk side by side to the conference room, neither of us saying anything. Pulling open the glass door, I wait for her to walk in.

"This is nice," she says, looking around at the big conference table that seats twenty. I walk over and hold out my hand to her to take a seat. I walk around the table and sit in front of her. "So official." She laughs. Putting the manila folder on the table and opening it, I hand her a copy across the table. "What is this?" she asks me before even reading. Her eyes go down, and then she looks up at me. "Custody agreement."

Twenty

Presley

"This is nice." I look around the conference room, holding my purse in front of me, feeling my whole body slowly shaking with nerves. He holds out his hand for me to take a seat, and I can't help but laugh nervously as I pull out one of the chairs. "So official." I look over at the other side of the table, watching him pull out his own chair. When I saw his name on the caller ID, I dropped the plate of fruit I was eating on my lap. It's been the longest days without him in them. Then seeing him, it just finally put me at ease with just one look at him. He opens the manila folder in front of him and hands me the white papers with black writing on it. "What is this?" I ask him, and my eyes go down to the paper in front of me.

My eyes go straight to two words. "Custody agreement." My eyes fly up to his, the shock running through me right now. This was the last thing that I thought he wanted to talk to me about. I thought we would sit down and hash out what happened. I thought I would be able to apologize for not calling him. I thought he would take me in his arms and hug me, but instead, it's my worst nightmare.

"Not a custody agreement." He holds up his hand to stop me from talking.

"Does this not read custody agreement?" I point at the words. My stomach flies to my throat, and I feel like I'm going to throw up. The back of my neck is tingling, and I feel suddenly hot. I went from feeling sad to anger to I don't even know how to explain it. Out of control.

"What I wanted to do is get everything down on paper so we can figure out what we will do," he says, and I can see his hand shaking. "Just so we are both covered, and neither of us is surprised by anything."

"I mean…" I put down the paper in front of me. "It's us, so I was just assuming that we would talk about things."

"And this is what we are doing," he confirms, and he looks down at the paper. "I just want to make sure that I have…"

"I will never, ever keep the baby from you," I assure him, and when he looks up at me, I see the worry in his eyes. "Bennett, you are the father of the baby." My mouth gets dry, and my nose starts to sting. "We are going to split custody fifty-fifty." I swallow the lump in my throat, saying the words. I knew that this was going to come. I mean, I even told myself that this is how it had to be. But then actually saying them out loud is another thing. I already was so in love with our child that I couldn't explain it, so the thought of not being there every day with him or her is a lot harder than I expected it to be.

"Which is why I think we should get things in writing so everything is out there." His finger starts to tap on the table, and I know that he's nervous.

"Sure," I say, looking back down at the papers in my hand.

"We can go through the points that I have," he says, and my eyes fly up to see him looking down at his own papers. When I walked out of the hospital room, I expected him to drive me home, but he left me with Clarabella. I had to bite my tongue on my way to keep from calling out to him. "I would like to be there for every doctor's appointment."

"Of course." It comes out harsher than I want it to be. "I would assume you would have been there anyway." My voice goes soft.

"I will take care of all medical bills that have to do with the baby," he states, and I shake my head.

"No," I say. "If there are any medical bills, it's split fifty-fifty."

He leans over and takes a pen out of the basket in the middle of the table to make notes on his paper. "Okay, I will change that." I can see him look at me, and I ignore the need to look up at him. "Have you decided if you are going to breastfeed or bottle feed?"

"I haven't given it any thought, to be honest." I look at him, and being here with him in this room is almost too much for me. "I'm assuming I'm going to breastfeed." I want to ask him if he is going to be taking my breast also, but I don't.

"If you decide to breastfeed, would you be open to pumping your milk so I can have some at my house?" He looks at me, and at this point, I just nod at him. "Great," he says, smiling at me, but I just look down.

I don't even know what else is discussed because, at this point, my head has shut it out. I push away from the table at the end of it. "Draft it up." I grab my purse and put the paper inside it. "And then I'll have my lawyer look at it." I nod at him, not saying another word because I have a feeling that the next words that come out of my mouth are not going to be good at all.

"I'll walk you out," he says, and I just shake my head.

"I'm fine." I turn to walk out of the room before he even has a chance to say anything else. I walk down the hallway with my head held high, even though it feels like I have a thousand pounds on my shoulders pushing me down. I keep it together the whole time even when I get in the car. I don't call anyone. I don't say anything. I'm just numb, and when I get home, I'm happy no one is there with me.

When I got home from the hospital, I expected to find my house pitch black, but instead, Shelby was there sitting on the porch steps waiting for us. She didn't really say much; neither of them did. They just made sure I was okay. They both spent the night, and the next day when I got up, I half expected to see a message from Bennett. But there was nothing. We had a meeting on my couch, and I didn't even fight them when they told me that I should just stay off my feet for a couple of days. I would do all the work from home. The only thing that I wouldn't be able to do is meet with potential clients. Every night one of them would come and stay with me, but I will be calling them as soon as I can speak without breaking down to tell them I would like to be alone.

I walk into the house, dumping my purse on the table, and head straight to my bedroom. I undress right after I start the shower. All I can hear in my head is his voice. All that I've been hearing in my head are the words I love you. Over and over again, day and night, it's always there.

Stopping to look in the mirror, I see the little bump that just started to form. If I didn't know that I was pregnant, I would think that I just overate. I put my hand on my stomach, something that I do all the time now. I step into the shower and put my face back, walking under the stream of the water. Only when I'm under the water do I let out the first sob. It rips through me like a lightning bolt. Stepping back, I put my hands over my face as I cry out. This right here is what I was afraid of all this time. This pain in my chest, and has been since he told me he loved me, is a pain that I can't even put into words. I want to say it's like a stabbing pain over and over, but it doesn't do it justice. Every single time my heart beats, it feels like another piece is cut off.

Getting out of the shower, I wipe my face, but the tears don't stop. Nothing will stop it, and I crawl into bed. Placing my head on the pillow and holding my stomach while I cry, this right here is what I was afraid of.

This right here is what I was avoiding this whole fucking time. The pain that I fought so hard not to feel, yet here I am, broken-hearted. I have no idea what to do or how to fix this.

Every single day, I get up and get out of bed, but I do it for the baby. I eat only because I know that the baby needs it. I go online every day to read everything it has on the baby at this stage. My whole world now revolves around this little baby who is my whole life. A baby who was conceived with love. A baby who will forever be a part of me and a part of Bennett. A baby who is now the only reason he wants to talk to me.

The room slowly gets dark, and even though I texted my sisters hours ago telling them not to come over tonight and that I was fine, I hear the front door open. "Baby momma," Clarabella calls out, and then I hear her feet coming closer and closer to my bedroom. "Are you sick?" she asks from the doorway. "Is it the baby?"

"I'm fine." I don't bother lifting my head, but I also don't bother hiding my face.

She sits on the bed next to me. "What's the matter?"

Everything, I almost say out loud. The fact that I love a man and can't tell him. The fact that I'm petrified of telling him with the notion that he'll leave me. The fact that even though I said that I had to leave him, actually doing it is killing my soul. But instead, I lie and try to tell myself that this is how it's supposed to be. "Nothing," I lie, and as I say it, the tears just continue to pour out. "I'll be fine," I whisper, hoping that tomorrow is a better day.

Twenty-One

Bennett

"I'll be back in about an hour," I tell Andrew as I walk out of my office. The phone starts to ring in my hand as I walk to the door. "Hello," I say after four rings, not even checking who it is.

"So I take it you're alive," Travis jokes to me as I chuckle, pushing open the office's front door and stepping out into the sunshine. The heat hits me right away as the sun burns down on me, making me shrug off my suit jacket.

"I'm alive," I assure him as I unlock the car door and get in, starting it right away. I toss my suit jacket on the passenger seat, the Bluetooth connecting right away, so I put my phone in the cupholder.

"It's been two weeks," he says, and I put my head back on the seat and close my eyes.

It's been sixteen days, to be exact, but who is counting? I almost say. "I know. I've been swamped with work," I huff. The only saving grace to all of this is that I'm in the middle of the biggest merger of my life. Two of the biggest tech companies are merging, and it's been all hands on deck since they came to us. It's a once-in-a-lifetime deal, and even though I spent over eight hours at the office, and I got home bone-dead tired, I still hated walking into my house. I didn't go anywhere but the bedroom. I sleep for a max of five hours, sometimes less, and when I'm done tossing and turning, I get up and just head to the office.

"I figured," he huffs. "I know this is weird, but we are having a birthday party for Charlotte, and Harlow said if you don't come, she's going to send her father to get you with his gun."

I can't help but laugh at that picture. "I'm not the one he wants to shoot." I make the joke, but the thought of going to the birthday party makes my stomach burn.

"Hey," he snaps. "He is starting to like me a bit more every day." He chuckles.

"Is that what you keep telling yourself?" I tap the steering wheel nervously, trying to think of an excuse.

"Is this your way of telling me you are trying to change the subject?" he comes back at me. I should have known he would see through the deflect.

"And here I was thinking I was so savvy." I laugh. "Will you take a maybe?" I finally say.

"Do I have a choice?" He chuckles.

"Why don't you ask Presley first and see how she feels? The last thing I want is for her to be uncomfortable." I close my eyes just saying her name. The ache in my chest is almost as strong as when I told her I loved her, which, according to Google and the article *How to Heal a Broken Heart,* I should already be learning to live with it. I also should point out that I'm still at step one, which is take time to grieve.

"You're a good, good man, Bennett," Travis says.

"Glad at least one of us thinks so," I say and pull out of the parking lot. My stomach fills with knots, knowing that in less than thirty minutes, I'm going to see her. "Let me know."

"Will do," he says. "Call you later." He disconnects.

I make my way over to the doctor's office, the whole time wondering if maybe I should get her something to drink or something to eat. I decide against it because I don't want her to feel like I'm overstepping. When I pull into the parking lot, I look around for her car, but I don't see it. I think about waiting in my car for her, but then I think it might make me look like I'm creeping on her. Getting out of the car, I put the phone in my front pocket while I roll up the sleeves to my white button-down shirt.

I run my hand through my hair when I step into the doctor's office. My eyes scan the room, and I see there is one person there sitting and reading a magazine. The receptionist looks up from her desk and smiles at me. "May I help you?"

"I'm meeting Presley Baker here," I explain, looking

at my watch and seeing that I'm ten minutes early.

"She hasn't arrived yet." She smiles at me. "If you would like to take a seat and wait for her."

"Thank you," I say, nodding to her. Walking over to one of the waiting room chairs, I take the phone out of my pocket and sit down. I put my left ankle on my right knee, pulling up her name on my text.

The last time I texted her was Saturday, and it was just to check in and see if she was okay. She responded a couple of hours later, telling me that she was fine. That was it. Luckily, I was in the office, and I had people around, so I couldn't dwell on it, but I'd be lying if I said that I didn't want to text her every day to ask her if she was okay. The worst thing with all of this is that she was also one of my best friends. I text her, my hand getting sweaty as I type the message.

Me: I'm here.

I exhale a deep breath, and the phone vibrates in my hand, and I see it's her.

Gorgeous: On my way!

I open Instagram on my phone, scrolling through while the food in my stomach starts to move around nervously. My body is on full alert for her. The door opens, and I look up, and everything in me almost does a sigh of relief when I see her. She takes off her sunglasses and looks around the room at me. I smile tightly at her, my cock already springing to action like he's going to be reunited with his best friend. She holds up her hand in a wave at me, walking over to the receptionist. Her black hair is perfectly styled and loose, her short, ruffle-sleeved, light pink one-piece dress she is wearing flows around her and reaches almost to her knees. The sash at her waist is tied on the side, and she is wearing a gold watch on one wrist and gold bracelets on the other. My eyes roam down to her heels that are sky high, and all that I can think of is man, she's fucking gorgeous.

She speaks to the receptionist, and I try to calm my breathing and my heart down. I would be lying to myself if I said I wasn't waiting for this moment for the past two days. I played it out over and over in my head. The plan was to be nonchalant with her. Play it cool and calm. Meanwhile, inside was frenzied and flustered. She turns around and comes my way, and I see that her blue eyes are darker than they usually are. I get up and stop myself before I'm about to lean over and kiss her cheek. "Hey," I greet, waiting for her to sit down before I sit back down.

"Hi," she says, putting her purse on her lap and crossing her legs. "Did you get here when you texted, or were you waiting long?" She turns to look at me, and I see her hands shaking a bit. I wonder if she is as nervous as I am.

"No." I shake my head. "Just when I texted." She nods at me, and it's the most awkward conversation we've ever had. "How are you doing?" I almost groan inwardly about how cringy that sounds.

"I'm doing good," she says, and the nurse saves us by calling her name. Presley gets up, and I follow her to the doctor's office.

"How are we feeling?" the nurse asks her while she waits for us to walk into the room and follows us in.

"Good," Presley confirms. "A bit tired." My neck tingles when I hear this. Is she not sleeping properly? Is she still having morning sickness? Is she eating properly? "I think it's mostly I was bored staying home." This is brand-new information to me as I thought she was working.

"It's totally normal. Your body is going through lots of changes," the nurse says. "If you want to change into the gown"—she points at the hospital gown on the examining table—"I'll be back to take your vitals."

I look around the room, seeing that there is no room for her to change. There is a desk in the corner with a computer on it, an exam table, and an ultrasound machine. "I'm going to wait outside while you change." My mouth goes dry as I picture her naked.

"I'll call you when I'm done," she says, not looking at me, and I see her blinking really fast. I pull open the door and step out into the hallway. I put my head on the brown door, closing my eyes and trying to tell myself that it's Presley, and no matter what happens, it's still just us.

"I'm done," she announces, and I open the door, stepping back into the room in time to see her hop onto the exam table. Her hands shake, and when I look at her, her eyes look like she has been crying. I'm about to ask her if everything is okay, but the doctor comes in.

I move to the side, uncertain of where to even stand. I hate this. I hate that we have become these two people who used to talk about everything and nothing, and now can't even say five words to each other without it being awkward.

"Afternoon," the doctor says, walking over to the table in the corner. She moves the mouse as the computer turns on, and she starts to read the notes. "So I see you went to the emergency room for bleeding?" she asks, looking over at Presley, who just nods at her. She raises her hand to the corner of her eye as she wipes away a tear. I put my hand in my pocket, my stomach filling with knots. "How has it been since?"

"I've been fine since. No blood," she answers the doctor.

"Is there a reason she was bleeding?" I ask the doctor, and she smiles sadly and shrugs her shoulders.

"It could be from a bunch of reasons or no reason at all," she states, turning to look over at the chart. "The good news is that it stopped, and I see that they heard the heartbeat." Presley smiles now when the doctor mentions the heartbeat, and it's a smile that lights up her whole face. It's a smile that makes me smile. "Okay, let's see what's going on in there."

Presley lies back on the table, and I move to the side of her but stay far enough away to not intrude on her space. I can see the doctor move the hospital gown up, and I force myself not to look at her. "This will be cold," the doctor says as she grabs the white bottle and then squeezes the gel on Presley's stomach.

She grabs the handpiece, picking it up and moving it around Presley's stomach. There in the middle of the screen, I see the baby. "There is the baby," she says, and I can't help but smile as I look down at Presley, who has one hand over her head and the other hand holding the hospital gown up in the middle of her chest. She isn't just smiling. She is beaming as she watches our child float around, going side to side.

"It's so strange that I can't feel any of that movement," she says softly.

"It usually happens at around eighteen to twenty weeks depending," the doctor says as she clicks buttons on the machine. She moves up and down on her stomach, side to side, and then she presses a button, and you hear the sound of swishing now. "That's a strong heartbeat. One hundred and forty-two beats a minute." She presses more buttons, and the machine spits out something.

"Is that a normal heartbeat?" I ask. "Or is it too high?"

"It varies from one hundred and ten to one hundred and sixty, depending on the child," she answers me.

She takes the wand off Presley, wiping off her stomach and then the machine before she turns the lights back on. Presley sits up now, letting her gown fall down. "Here are some more pictures." She hands them to Presley, who just looks down at them. "Do you have any questions for me?" the doctor says, rolling back to the desk and typing things in.

"I have a question." I hold up my hand as if I'm in school and take out my phone.

"Yeah, you can still have sex." The doctor laughs, and I chuckle nervously at that comment.

"That wasn't the question, but good to know." I nod at her and look over at Presley, who just rolls her lips. "I was reading online that with the bleeding, the pregnancy could be a high risk?"

"From what I see, I don't think so," the doctor says. "But it's still too early to tell. My advice is to listen to your body." She turns to look at Presley. "If your body is saying you are tired, sit down and rest. If you have all the energy and want to take a walk, then do that."

"Good to know," Presley says, putting her hand on her stomach. "I've been staying off my feet ever since the hospital, only going in to work twice a week but mainly just sitting."

"You are doing everything you need to do." The doctor gets up. "I'll see you in a month, and if you have any questions, you can call me." She walks out of the room, and I look back at Presley.

"Are you okay?" I ask, and she nods her head.

"It's still crazy that the baby moves so much, and I don't even feel anything." She laughs. "Even if I put my hand on my stomach, I don't even feel a flutter." She gets down off the exam table. "Here you go." She hands me the pictures. Our fingers graze each other, and it tingles all up my arm. I look at her to see if she is as affected as I am. But she turns away just as quickly. "You can look at them while I change."

Twenty-Two

Presley

"Here you go," I say, getting off the exam table and handing him the pictures of the ultrasound. Our fingers graze each other, and it almost feels like an electric shock runs through my body. I quickly move my hand away and turn so he doesn't see the tears that form in my eyes. "You can look at them while I change," I say softly, looking over to my dress that I hung up on the hook.

"I'll wait for you outside," he says, and I wait until the sound of the door clicks shut behind him before I walk over to the chair and sit down. My breathing is coming in pants now.

"Fuck, fuck, fuck," I say over and over again as I count to twenty, and when that doesn't work, I count to fifty. Ever since I walked into this office and saw him, my whole body has been on high alert. It's been over two weeks since I've seen him, and I thought for sure it wouldn't bother me as much as it did the last time, but I was wrong. The pain was, in fact, even worse than before, which I didn't think was humanly possible. How could you hurt more than you did before? There were days when I felt like someone beat the shit out of me. Every single bone in my body hurt. Every single step that I took felt heavier and heavier. The only thing that kept me going was the baby. It was the only joy in my life. I would spend hours online searching about things happening at this time.

I get up, making my way over to my dress that I wore just for him. My hand shakes when I take it down and put it over my head. Tying the sash around my waist, the small little stomach that has started to come out is making it uncomfortable for me to button my pants, so I'm often in dresses. I smile as I put my hand on my stomach. "He loves you so much," I can't help but say as I wipe the lone tear that comes out of my eye. Every single time I miss him, I tell the baby how much he loves her or him. Which happens about ten times an hour at this point. During one night of restlessness, I got so in my head that the heartache I was feeling would be breaking the baby's heart, so I spent five hours looking if this could or would actually happen.

I grab my purse, not even bothering to look at myself in the mirror. If anything, I'll just blame it on hormones. I've been using this excuse for the past two weeks, and

I'm sure my sisters are ready to call me out on it. When I pull open the door, I'm surprised to see him leaning against the wall, waiting for me while he looks at the pictures in his hand. "Oh," I say. "I didn't think you would be here."

His eyebrows shoot together. "Where else would I be?"

"I don't know," I reply, walking out. "I thought you would be in the waiting room," I mumble. I stop and make another appointment, and he takes out his phone to put it in his calendar. He gets a pair of scissors from the receptionist and cuts his picture off, handing me one.

"I think I'm going to get one frame for each month," he says as we walk out, and I can't help but smile and look over at him. "That's not too much, right?"

"I've already started the ultrasound montage on the bedroom wall," I admit to him as our walking slows down the closer we get to our cars. "This is me," I say, pointing at the car.

"Oh, yeah," he replies and looks as if he wants to say something, but instead, he nods at me. "Let me know if you need anything."

"Will do," I say, swallowing the lump and walking over to my car. I don't bother looking to see if he got in his car as I drive away. I think about going home, but if I do that, I'll just be sitting in the middle of the couch, so instead, I head to the office.

I park next to Clarabella's car and walk inside. I can hear them talking as I walk down the hallway. "Hola," I say, trying to be as chipper as I can as I stick my head into Clarabella's office. Seeing Shelby is lying down on her couch with her hand on her head.

"What are you doing here?" Clarabella asks me, and I glare at her.

"Last I checked"—I look around—"I work here."

"Didn't you have a doctor's appointment?" Shelby opens her eyes and looks over at me.

"I just came from there, and the doctor said that I need to listen to my body." I sit in one of the empty chairs. "So my body said to come to work."

"Was Bennett there?" Clarabella asks as she leans back in her chair.

"Well, he is the father, so yes, he was there," I confirm, ignoring the way my stomach flips and flops when I think about him. The minute I saw him, I couldn't even move. He looked even more handsome than he did the last time, and I didn't think it was possible. His sleeves were rolled up like they always are, and my eyes stared at them, thinking about the times he used to hold me. *I took him for granted.*

"Did you tell him how you felt, or are you still a dumbass?" Clarabella asks me, and all I can do is flip her the bird.

"What were you guys talking about?" I change the subject, and she just snickers at me.

"When are you going to be able to meet with clients?" Shelby huffs as she now gets up from lying down. "I don't know how much longer I can do this." She closes her eyes, and now it's my turn to laugh.

"What happened?" I ask and look at Clarabella, who

just shakes her head and laughs.

"I met with a couple today who got engaged after three weeks." Shelby puts both hands up. "I have food in my fridge older than that relationship." She shakes her head. "Anyway, they are walking around the venue, and the guy decides that today at this moment, while choosing how they would put tables, to ask her what her number is."

"If I was there, I would have told her not to answer," Clarabella deadpans.

I gasp. "Did she actually answer?" My eyes go big as I look at Shelby, who rolls her lips and nods her head.

"She wasn't the problem," Shelby says. "She laughed at him and was like six, and she thought she was the one with the high number."

"Oh my God." My hand goes to my mouth.

"Yeah, but turns out he's over one hundred. He stopped counting, apparently, because after one hundred, it's redundant!" Shelby shares, and all I can do is stare at her while Clarabella laughs.

"So they aren't getting married?" I ask, and this is when Clarabella starts to slap her desk in a fit of laughter.

"No," Shelby says. "She thought it was the most romantic thing in the world that he would choose her forever."

"Damn," I say. "Isn't it like a rule to never tell your number?"

"I told Luke," Clarabella says. "It was more than five."

"I mean, Ace knew before we got married," Shelby

declares and then tilts her head to the side. "Why? What's your number?"

"Um," I say, thinking about lying to them but knowing that they would probably see right through me.

"Oh my God," Clarabella says. "You dirty dog."

"Hardly," I say, bracing myself. "One." The minute I say the number, you could hear a fucking pin drop.

"You're lying!" That's the first thing Clarabella shouts to me, and I shake my head.

"How is that possible?" Shelby gasps. "You were on Tinder."

"So?" I snap. "Not everyone that goes on Tinder is there for sex."

"So, you went out on dates," Clarabella says.

"I did, but that didn't mean I had to sleep with them." I get up now.

"You're a dumbass," Shelby says, getting up. "You spent the past twelve years sleeping with one man who you are now having a child with, and you're going to tell me that you don't have any feelings for him."

"Of course, I have feelings for him," I say, swallowing. *I love him,* my head screams. "But I also know that he wants the whole package with a white picket fence and June Cleaver in the kitchen." I ignore the sting that starts in my eyes. "So it is what it is. Now I'm going to go and see if I can get something to eat."

I turn to walk out. "Or you can text Bennett and ask him to go out and eat with you and tell him." I don't even listen to the rest of what Shelby has to say before she finishes her sentence.

Every single Saturday like clockwork, the phone rings, and I see his name. And every single second after that for the next three days, I can't get my head together. It's only on the third Saturday that there is no text, and I know that it's because we are both going to be at Charlotte's birthday party.

I spend way too much time picking out my outfit, making sure that my makeup is perfect, and when I slip on the dark blue sleeveless A-line cotton dress, I smile. I want to tell myself that I'm smiling because I'm going to see the family today, but deep down, I know I'm smiling because I'm going to see Bennett. I also ignore the thought of him sitting down and talking to me.

I park my car and get the gift from the truck when Harlow's brother, Reed, walks out the front door. "Hey there," he says, holding up his hand to wave at me as he smiles. "My father sent me out here to grab the gift and told me that if I didn't take it from you, he's going to kick my ass."

I can't help but laugh. "Well, aren't you a gentleman," I say, kissing his cheek when he comes closer. "How are you?" I ask as he grabs the box from me, and we walk up the steps.

As soon as I step foot inside the house, I see the chaos. There has to be over fifty people here. "Why didn't we do this at the venue?" I ask Travis when he sees me.

"We wanted an intimate affair." He rolls his eyes. "By the way," he says and looks down, and I can see that he's nervous about something. "I just wanted to give you a heads-up that Bennett is coming."

I laugh. "I would assume so. He's your best friend."

"He might also bring someone," he says, and my whole body turns to ice. My stomach sinks to my feet, and I feel tingles running all through my body. I also think I'm going to be sick. "I can tell him not to come."

"No." I shake my head and put the biggest fake smile on my face I've ever put. "It's fine." I look around. "I'm going to go and see if I can find Mom." He takes one look at me and lets me go. If I stayed there any longer, I might have burst into tears.

I walk out of the house toward the backyard, and the only thing going through my head is getting the fuck out of here. I look down and walk to the side of the fence, hoping no one stops me. I'll just text Clarabella and tell her that I wasn't feeling well.

The minute I escape the yard without being seen, I walk toward my car. My head is bent, and I don't even see him before I come face-to-face with him and his date.

Twenty-Three

Bennett

"Are you sure this is okay?" Clarissa asks from beside me as we walk on the grass toward the backyard.

"Of course." I smile over at her. "I called ahead and asked just to make sure." I look down and then look up again, and I see her walking toward me. My heart stops in my chest when I see her, just like every single time. She doesn't see me watching her as she makes her way closer to me. It takes a couple of seconds before she looks up, and I see that her eyes are a darker blue. Usually, when something is bothering her, they turn that color. "Hey." I hold up my hand as we get close enough.

"Hi." She puts on the fakest smile that I've ever seen on her.

"Were you leaving?" I ask, looking at her with her purse in her hand.

"Oh, no." She shakes her head. "Forgot my phone in the car."

"Do you want me to go get it?" I point back at her car with my thumb.

She shakes her head again. "No, that's okay." She looks down. "You should go in there." Neither of us says anything else, and it gets super awkward. I don't want to walk away from her. I was hoping that since we were going to be seeing each other, we would sit down and talk.

"Hi," Clarissa interrupts us and extends her hand to Presley. "I'm Clarissa," she says, smiling.

"I'm Presley," Presley responds, extending one hand, and I see that the hand that is holding her purse, her knuckles are white. "Nice to meet you." She shakes Clarissa's hand for a couple of seconds. "If you will excuse me, I want to get back in there before they run out of food."

My eyebrows pinch together at this comment because there is no way that any of their parties will run out of food. Ever. Presley avoids making eye contact with me as she walks around Clarissa and goes to her car. I take an extra second to watch her, and if it was up to me, I would wait for her to go to her car and come back, but Clarissa says, "Shall we get in there?" I look back at her.

"Yes." I nod my head and turn to walk into the backyard. The minute the gate opens, showing me the party, my mouth almost hits the floor. There have to be about four or five bouncy things set up with kids running all over the place. There are not one but three barbecues set up side by side on the other side of the yard. There is also a small tented area where I see Harlow's grandparents sitting. Her grandfather is the picture of a cowboy. I have never ever seen him without his hat on. Even at their wedding, he wore it. Also one look from him when he's mad, and you know that he'll whip your ass.

"Now this is a birthday party." Clarissa laughs from beside me, and she is not wrong.

"Obviously, it's a 'go big or go home' situation." I chuckle as my eyes roam around the yard to see if I see Travis or Harlow anywhere. I also stand close to the gate, secretly waiting for Presley to come back to make sure she is okay. But Clarissa starts to walk farther into the yard, and I have to follow her.

"There you are," I hear from the side and see Travis walking over to me. "Was wondering when you would get here," he says with his lips tight between his clenched teeth.

I fold my arms over my chest. "You just wanted someone in your corner."

He scoffs at me. "No." He shakes his head. "I have Billy." He motions with his head toward Harlow's grandfather. "And I'm sure Olivia wouldn't let them shoot me."

"Clarissa," I introduce, looking over at her. "This is my best friend, Travis."

"Nice to meet you," Clarissa says to him.

"Did you get something to drink?" Travis asks us.

"We just got here," I say, and I look around, trying to see if Presley came back in. "I'll go and get something to drink." I make the excuse to get away. "What do you want to drink?" I ask Clarissa.

"A water is fine," she says, and I nod at her.

"Whatever you do." I lean in and try to whisper, but with so many people here there is no such thing as whispering. "Don't drink the sweet tea."

Travis laughs. "That sweet tea is how I slept with Harlow on my would-be wedding night."

I shake my head. "You can explain that to Clarissa," I say, laughing as I walk through the yard and making my way inside to see if maybe she is there.

As soon as I step inside, I see even more people. I knew Harlow had a big family, but having them all together is over the top. I zigzag through so many people, finally seeing Harlow. "Hey, have you seen Presley?" I ask, looking around to see if she is sitting somewhere, and I don't see her.

"She went to the bathroom," she says to me, and she's about to say something else when someone calls her name. "Shit," she says, rushing away from me.

I walk to the bathroom and see the door closed. I'm mentally deciding if I stay by the bathroom like a Peeping Tom or just go back to the living room and wait when the door is pulled open. She gasps when she sees me standing here. "Oh my God, you scared the shit out of me," she says, and I love what she is wearing. The blue of the dress makes her eyes pop even more.

"Sorry." I smile at her. "I was just seeing if you were

okay." The echoing of my heart beating is now filling my ears. My stomach feels like it's moving to my throat. "I didn't text you today." My head is yelling at me to shut the fuck up, but my mouth is deciding that today is a good day to have word vomit. "I know I usually text you, but I figured since we would be here, it would be better to ask you in person." *I was also wondering if you wanted to sit down and talk,* I want to add, but I don't.

"The baby is fine," she says, looking at me, and I can see that her walls are up. Her eyes are giving me nothing, but they look a little red.

"Okay, that is good to know," I say, putting my hands in my pockets before I do something stupid like wrap my arm around her waist and kiss her just like I've been dreaming about for the past fucking month. "But I was asking if you are okay?"

"I'm totally okay." She swallows. "You should get back to your date."

I just stare at her as I let her words replay in my head twice. "Not that it's any of your business." My heart breaks saying that because I want it to be her business. I want her to fucking care. "But she's just a friend." I turn and walk away before I say something I will regret.

I grab a couple of water bottles and walk out of the house. I look around for Clarissa but see that she's talking to Harlow's cousins. I walk over to one of the chairs at the far side where no one is at and sit down. I put my head back and close my eyes as I exhale. "What are you doing, hiding out?" I hear Travis and look up to see him walking toward me.

"No," I deny, shaking my head. "Just…" I put the water bottles down by my feet and then lean my elbows on my knees. "It's just fucking…" I can't even say the words. They all get stuck in my throat. "I'm dying inside," I finally say to him, and I really fucking wish that I wasn't here right now. "Every fucking day, I expect my feelings for Presley to get weaker, but then I see her, and it's just so much stronger." The tightness in my chest makes it even harder for me to breathe.

"I don't know what to say," he says softly, and I look over at him. "I wish I had the answer for you."

"Well, well, well," I hear and look over and see Clarabella and Shelby coming our way. "What are you two doing?" Shelby asks.

"Just enjoying the party." Travis covers for me as the two of them now stand in front of me.

"I have to say." Clarabella glares at me. "Took balls to bring a date today."

"A date?" I say again, confused. "She's not my date." I shake my head. "We went to school together. She's my co-worker from out of town. She was supposed to go back home to her *husband* yesterday, but that changed." I look at both of them as they stare at me with their mouths hanging open now. "We are finalizing the merger tomorrow, so she stayed, and instead of leaving her all alone in a hotel room, I invited her here."

"So you're not dating her?" Shelby asks just for clarification, and I can't help but stare at her dumbfounded.

"Did you miss the point where she is going back home to her husband?" I glare at her. "Why the hell would I bring a fucking date here?" I throw my hands up in frustration.

"Well, I don't know." Clarabella rolls her eyes. "Maybe because you can," she huffs. "Maybe to make Presley see that you've moved on."

"Yeah, moved on," I say sarcastically. "I've moved on in what, a month."

"What the hell were we supposed to think?" Shelby shrieks. "You show up with a woman. We assume that this is a date."

"So you guys think, not only am I dating after being in love with your sister for—I don't know—almost my whole life, that I'm going to bring her here to your family's party." I glare at both of them. "Wow."

"I want to go on the record as saying I knew he wouldn't do it," Travis cuts in, and I side-eye him.

"I would never do that to her," I say softly.

"She just…" Shelby says softly. "She's working it out."

"But is she?" I ask, getting up. "Because she seems to be fine."

"She just needs space," Clarabella explains, and I snap. "She cares for you."

"Oh, goody," I say, clapping my hands. "She cares for me. Just what I wanted to hear."

"Okay, maybe that wasn't the right word to use," Shelby hisses, looking at Clarabella.

"You know what? None of this is right." I hold up my hand. "Nothing about this is right." I bend down and grab the bottles of water. "Now if you guys will excuse me, I have to go back to my friend." I look at her sisters. "Not my date."

They both fold their arms over their chests and roll their eyes. "Suddenly, he's a comedian."

"Whatever," I huff and start to walk away before turning. "Also, can someone go and make sure she is okay?"

"Who do you want us to check on?" Clarabella rolls her lips. "Your baby momma or your date?"

Travis snickers, and all I can do is flip her the bird as I turn and walk away. "We love you!" Clarabella shouts.

"Great," I mumble under my breath. "Well, at least one of you does," I say, making my way over to Clarissa and forcing myself not to look around for her. The whole time, all I can do is hear her sister's voice play over and over in my head. *"She cares for you."*

Twenty-Four

Presley

$\mathcal{I}$ sit in the chair in the backyard, counting down the minutes until I can leave without it being obvious that I'm leaving because I'm uncomfortable with Bennett bringing a date.

I look over and see Harlow chatting with Clarissa. My stomach burns, and I bring the bottle of water to my lips, wishing it was something stronger. The minute I was introduced to her, I wanted to get the fuck out of there. Forget that I sat in the car for five minutes talking myself out of it.

What did I do? I told myself fuck him, this is my family, and then walked in and went to the bathroom, where I cried a bit and then made sure I looked semi okay before opening the door. I almost shit myself when I saw him. Seeing him standing there in his black jeans and the cotton T-shirt with his arms showing just had everything inside me light up. All I wanted was to jump into his arms. All I wanted was his lips on mine. All I wanted was for him to be mine. But he was moving on.

"Are you sulking?" Clarabella comes over and sits next to me. Followed by Shelby, who sits on the other side of me.

"This is called relaxing," I inform them, taking a sip of the water. "And staying off my feet."

"I call it if looks could kill," Shelby says and motions with her chin toward Clarissa who has fit in with everyone. She smiles, laughs, and she's pretty. I hate her.

"I'm not looking at anything." I turn my head, looking at the other side.

"You wanted this," Shelby reminds me, and I make a mistake of looking at the other side and seeing Bennett sitting with the guys. He sits in the middle with Travis on one side and Ace on the other side. Luke sits next to Ace. Ace says something, and the four of them laugh, and I can't help the lone tear that escapes my eye. "You wanted him to be free."

"Yes," I say, swallowing the lump in my throat. "Well, now he's moved on obviously." I hold up my hand. I watched Clarissa's face when I said my name to see if there was a flicker there that she knew who I was, but there was nothing. She was oblivious to who I was, and I just had more questions in my head. Did he not mention the baby? Did he not mention that he was with me for so long? Did his past not come up? How long have they been together? Did they date when he was in college? Have they dated before? I was making myself literally sick with all of these questions, and all I wanted to do was go home and be in the safety of my house.

"You are so full of shit," Clarabella snaps. "You can't even try to tell me that this doesn't bug you." I don't answer her because I can't. The lump in my throat is so big that nothing will come out. "You can't tell me that him being here with another woman doesn't bug you."

"One day, he is really going to move on," Shelby says, and I look over at her confused. "And then what?"

I'm about to answer her when I see my mother coming over to us. The smile on her face is anything but friendly. It's almost as if it's a glare. "Oh, fuck," Shelby says when she finally sees our mother. "That smile is the same one she had on when Clarabella ran away from her wedding."

"I didn't fucking run," Clarabella defends between clenched teeth. "I left quickly."

"So this is where you are?" My mother looks around to make sure no one is around us before the smile disappears off her face. "What are you doing?"

"What does it look like she's doing?" Shelby answers her. "She's training to be an Olympic athlete in gymnastics." She rolls her eyes. "Obviously."

"You," my mother says between clenched teeth, "go make sure your husband is okay."

"He's fine," Shelby says. "He's sitting with the other husbands and Presley's baby daddy." I swear if steam could come out of my mother's ears, now would be the time.

"How can you allow this to happen?" My mother looks at me for a second before turning and smiling at people she sees looking at us.

"How can I allow what to happen?" I ask. Today has been a day, and I'm emotionally worn out. I'm mentally exhausted, and to top it all off, I just want to sit down and cry.

"He brings these random women to events," she says with a smile and through clenched teeth.

"Oh, God, Mom," Shelby groans.

"He's never brought a woman to any event," Clarabella says, and I just look over at her. "Except today, but..."

"But nothing," my mother says. "How are you going to feel when he parades these women in front of your child?"

"Considering that my child is currently in my uterus and has no concept of anything that is happening here." I do a circle with my hand. "I'm going to say that for now it's fine."

"What about when he gets serious with a girl?" my mother says, and my stomach gets tight. "Then what?"

"Mom, she doesn't care." Shelby repeats my words, and I want to snap at her. "This is what she wants."

No, it's not. I almost scream, but instead I get up. "Mom"—I kiss her cheek—"thank you for looking out for me." I blink away the tears. "But let's not jump the gun. This might be their first date."

"Or maybe not," Shelby says.

"I'm going to head out," I respond. "Will you guys tell Travis and Harlow goodbye for me?"

Clarabella gets up. "I'll come with you."

"No." I shake my head. "I don't want to draw too much attention to myself."

"Will you call me when you get home?" Shelby asks, getting up, and I nod at her.

I turn to hug my mother. "Thanks for looking out for me, Mom." I put my head on her shoulder. "And for making me my favorite chicken potpie tomorrow."

"Ohhh, I want some of that also," Shelby says. "I'm coming."

"It's Sunday," Clarabella says. "You guys know that it's my special time."

"I can't believe you still do naked Sunday." I shake my head. "You are married to him and go to sleep with him every night."

"It keeps the romance alive." She shrugs, and I laugh, putting my head down and walking up the steps to the house. I step inside, counting down the seconds until I can grab my purse and escape from this. I quietly walk out of the house and head to my car, not letting out that sigh of relief until I'm finally driving away from the house.

Parking the car in the driveway, I grab my purse and make my way inside. Dropping everything on the floor as soon as I walk in, I kick off my shoes and go to the fridge. My hand snatches the apple juice as I walk over to get a glass. I don't know what it is but ever since I found out I was pregnant, it's the only thing I want to drink. It also has to be cold and crisp, pouring the glass almost to the top before turning and walking over to the couch.

I take a sip before sitting down and turning on the television. *This is my life now*, I think as I curl my feet under me. I'm scrolling Netflix when I feel a little flutter in my stomach, and I stop. "I felt that," I say to the empty room, my heart speeding up faster. I take another sip of the apple juice, and it happens again. I just squeal. "Oh my God, the baby is moving, and I feel it." I get up, and my first thought is to call Bennett, but I stop myself.

"What about when he gets serious with a girl?" My mother's voice replays in my head. *"Then what?"*

I sit back down, putting my hand on my stomach.

"You wanted this." Shelby's voice now replays. *"You wanted him to be free."*

"You are so full of shit." Clarabella's voice cuts in. *"You can't even try to tell me that this doesn't bug you. You can't tell me that him being here with another woman doesn't bug you."*

I put my head back on the couch, playing the whole night over and over again in my head. I don't know when I get up and walk upstairs, but I know the next morning when I walk down the stairs, there is only one decision left for me. I walk to my phone and then walk over to the kitchen island.

Me: Can you call me when you have a minute? Everything is fine; just wanted to ask you something.

I press send before I chicken out and place it on the counter in front of me. My eyes watch it to see if he's read it. I wait to see the three little dots come up, and they don't. Maybe he's with Clarissa? The thought alone makes me physically ill as I run to the bathroom and throw up.

Turning on the cold water, I wash my face before walking back out. Grabbing the phone, I text my sisters.

Me: Emergency Code, whatever, get your ass to Mom's house. Clarabella, wear clothes.

As soon as I send the text, I turn and run up the stairs, grabbing another summer dress. This one is a baby-blue floral halter top. It has an elastic waist and goes down to my ankles. I can hear my phone pinging downstairs while I brush my teeth. I slip on the brown flip-flops, and my heart speeds up when I pick up my phone, wondering if Bennett answered me back, but I see it's just my sisters.

Clarabella: I'm already dressed and out the door.

Shelby: What do you mean code whatever? There are colors for a reason.

Clarabella: It must be almost dire if she is asking us to meet her at Mom's house.

Shelby: This is true unless it's an ambush.

Clarabella: An ambush for what?

Shelby: She might want us to have a kid with her.

Clarabella: You think they are going to steal your eggs and ovaries?

I can't even with my sisters, so I just shake my head.

Me: Just meet me at Mom's. No one wants anyone's eggs. I need help.

I press send, walking to the door as the phone vibrates in my hand.

Shelby: She's dying, she has to be. She's never asked for help.

Clarabella: Oh my God, maybe she needs a kidney. I don't know if I can give her one of mine. What if my kids need it?

Shelby: Now you're having a kid.

Clarabella: Well, not this minute, but what if they need one and I don't have it?

I don't even bother answering the rest of the texts; I just get to my mother's house. I walk inside and find her in the kitchen. "You're early," she says as she rolls out the dough for the potpie. "What happened?"

"I'm going to wait until…" I'm starting to say when the door opens.

"I'm here," Shelby says and then the door opens again.

"I'm here with all my organs," Clarabella says. "And I'm not sharing." They both walk into the kitchen. "Mom, you can't make me share."

"What the hell are you guys talking about?" my mother says, confused. "Why are you all here?"

"I told them to come," I explain, and now I can't even stay put as I start to pace the kitchen. "I don't know how to say this." I shake my hands, the nerves making them shake.

"She does need a kidney." Shelby leans in and whispers to Clarabella.

"I don't need a kidney!" I shout, throwing up my hands. "I think I'm in love with Bennett!" I shout, and the whole room goes silent. I don't even think they're breathing. I look at my sisters who look at me, and then to my mother, whose eyes look like they are going to come out of her head. I am so nervous that I put my hand to my stomach, and I feel like I'm about to throw up again.

"No shit," Clarabella says, shaking her head. "I got dressed for this?"

"Oh my God," my mother says, putting her hands on her cheeks.

Shelby slaps her arm. "I think what Clarabella meant to say was wow, this is great news. But now the question is, what are you going to do about it?"

I look down at the floor and then I look up. "I have no fucking clue."

Twenty-Five

Bennett

The conference room is full. Every single chair is taken as we work through the merger. Bottles of water are all over the table, and my neck is killing me from staying in the same spot for the past ten hours. I look up and see all of the tired faces. "We are in the home stretch, people." They all look up at me. "Why don't we take ten?"

There are so many sighs of relief when I say that, it takes a second more for all of them to push away from the table and stretch their legs. I get up and go into my office. My head is throbbing softly, my back is killing me, and all I want to do is close my eyes. I spent zero minutes sleeping last night. Zero. I lean back in the chair and close my eyes. "I guess you're as tired as I am?" My eyes flutter open to see Clarissa leaning against the doorjamb.

"Hopefully we can get this done in the next hour and then you can go back home." I rock in my chair back and forth.

"Music to my ears." She smiles. "Thank you for inviting me yesterday. It was a blast." She huffs, "And I'm still full."

I laugh at that because, knowing Harlow and her family, she probably had to eat five times the food just to please them. "Not a problem," I say. "Hope you had fun."

"It was so much fun." She pushes off from the doorjamb. "I'm going to go and step outside and see if I can spot the sun."

I close my eyes again for just a second. Maybe bringing her to the birthday party wasn't such a great idea. It was only when I got there and I found out that Presley thought she was my date did it really make me second-guess inviting her. It also didn't help that Mrs. Baker spent the majority of the day glaring at me from across the room. That mixed in with the conversation with her sisters and then finding out that she dipped out early, I was a fucking mess.

"Five minutes!" I hear someone yell from the hallway and open my eyes, grabbing my phone to see if I missed anything. My heart stops when I see that I have a text from her sent about eight hours ago.

Gorgeous: Can you call me when you have a minute?

Everything is fine; just wanted to ask you something.

My fingers are typing her back at the same time that I hold my breath.

Me: Still at work, will call you as soon as I leave.

My foot starts to move up and down when I see the three dots pop up and then another message comes in.

Gorgeous: Okay. I'll wait for your call.

I look down at the screen. Since when has she ever waited for my call? "Okay, people," I hear from the hallway. "Let's get this show on the road." I get up from my chair, bringing my phone with me, just in case she texts me back and it's actually an emergency. The nerves take over the pit of my stomach. I sit back in my chair in the conference room.

"Let's get the show on the road," I urge, trying to pump everyone up. I look around the table and see all of them focusing on the papers in front of them. "As soon as we are done with this, we can take the next two days off." All of the heads snap to look at me. "That's what I like to see," I joke. "Motivation."

"If we finish this in an hour," the other partner says, "I'll add two days to that."

"If we finish in forty-five minutes," I counter. "We get the week." I clap my hands. "Now let's go."

My team does not play when it comes to time off. It takes us less than forty-five minutes to finish the rest of the merger. All notes have been entered, and when I get up forty-four minutes later with the file in my hand, I walk out, proud of the work that we just poured three weeks into. I huff out as I walk out of the conference room and head to my office. Putting the file down and grabbing my things, I am one of the last ones to walk out of the office.

It's as dark now as when I got here this morning. I slip into the car and start it, pulling up Presley's name. Everything inside me is trembling, everything from my hands to my heart. The sound of ringing fills the car, and she picks up after two rings. "Hello?" Her voice comes out softly.

"Hey," I say, my voice trembling. "Sorry, I just got out of the office." I pull away from the office and make my way home. "We were finalizing a merger."

"Oh, yeah, no worries," she says. "I was…" She stops talking. "Um…" I can tell she's nervous about something. "I was wondering if we could talk."

"Um, yeah. I'm on my way home now. How is tomorrow?" I suggest, and I pull up to my house and see her sitting outside on my steps. I stop, and she looks at me. Her hair is loose and she is wearing a baby-blue flowered dress. She looks beautiful and she glows.

"How about now?" she asks, and I pull into the driveway. She disconnects the phone, and I get out, leaving my phone in the car.

"How long have you been here?" I ask, walking up the steps.

"I want to say not long," she says and then looks over at the bag of food beside her. "But Clarabella had to drop off food." She wrings her hands.

"Is everything okay?" I ask, suddenly worried that something happened and she wanted to do this face-to-face.

"Yeah." She gets up, and the dress falls to her ankles. "It's just, I kind of have something to talk to you about, and if I didn't come here, I don't know if I would have the courage tomorrow."

"Why don't we get you out of the heat?" I tell her, walking past her and ignoring the way that my head is spinning. I open the door and step in with her following me. I turn on the lights in the kitchen. "Do you want some water?"

"No." She shakes her head. "If I drink I'm probably going to throw up." She puts her hand to her stomach.

"Do you want to sit?" I ask, and she just looks at me.

"How much time do we have?" she asks, and I tilt my head to the side. "Like, is your date coming over?"

"I'm not dating anyone," I tell her. "Clarissa works for the firm, and she's here to help with the merger. She is happily married to her husband."

"What?" she gasps. "Why didn't you lead with that yesterday?"

"Why would you think I was on a date to begin with?" I counter her with my question.

"Because you showed up with her?" She throws her hands in the air. "What else would I think?"

"I would think that you would know how I feel about you." I put my hands on my hips.

"About that." She tries to joke, but I see her lower lip tremble. "I think I messed up." She says the words as if she is in pain. "Oh, God," she says as she puts her hand to her forehead. "This is a lot harder than I thought it would be." My feet stick to the floor in my kitchen with an island between us. My head is going around and around as I try to figure out what the fuck she was saying. "When my father died…" She starts and then I can see the tears form in her eyes and she wipes them away. "I saw my mother go through every single day with something missing. She would pretend she was okay, she still does, but at night when she would climb into bed, I would hear her talking to him through the wall. She would literally go over her whole day." I can't even imagine how I would have handled that. "And then in the morning, it would be like it never happened."

"Gorgeous," I say to her, but she shakes her head and holds up her hand.

"If you interrupt me, I won't say what I need to say," she says. "What you deserve to know. I vowed I would never fall in love because losing it would have broken me." She wipes off her cheeks, but the tears keep rolling down them. "I just never wanted to rely on someone so much that if they left, half of me would leave with them." She chuckles. "And then, well, my siblings didn't help that at all. Watching Travis, Clarabella, and Shelby getting their hearts broken, and here I was with the only guy I've ever been with." Her voice shakes. "So I fought it because if I said how I felt, it would be taken away from me. It would be ripped from me, and then I would be just like my mother." She looks down, and I see her hands shaking. "Bennett, I won't be able to survive without you." She smiles through her tears. "The minute that I admit what I'm so scared to admit, it'll be the end of us, and I don't think I can survive. These last weeks have been hell, one thousand percent the worst days of my life, and if it wasn't for the baby, I don't know where I would be. Last night at home, I felt the baby kick for the first time," she says with a beaming smile, and I can't help the smile that fills my face. "At first, I thought it was in my head, but then I drank more apple juice, and it was not in my head." Her smile fades. "And all I wanted to do was call you. All I wanted was for you to be there with me. All I wanted was…" She trails off.

I swallow down the lump in my throat as the words she's just said spin around in my head. "In the hospital room, I told you."

"You told me you loved me at the same time that I was scared to lose our child," she snaps. "The whole reason I didn't call you was because I thought you would hate me if anything happened to the baby." Oh my God, it's my turn to put my hands in front of my mouth. How could she even be thinking that?

"I would never…" I start to say to her, but she cuts me off.

"I know that, but can you imagine being the reason you lost the baby?" she says softly. "That day you were so happy and then…" She trails off.

"What are you saying to me?" I ask, wanting to hear it, wanting her to admit what I've known in my heart this whole time.

She takes the biggest inhale I've ever seen. Her chest rising and falling, her hands shaking. "I'm saying that I'm in love with you." She puts her hand to her mouth to stop the sob. "I'm saying that I love you, and I'm in love with you. I'm saying that I want this, me and you. This is what I want." She shakes her head and looks down at her hands. "And I get that I might be too late and that you may have moved on." She looks back up at me. "I don't even know what I would do if the roles were reversed." She smiles sadly. "I mean, my sisters would probably burn down your house and put fire ants in your bed."

I can't help but laugh at that. "I can only imagine."

"So this is it." She extends her hands to the sides. "Me admitting what I should have told you in the hospital room."

"Why now?" I ask.

"Well, one, you brought a date to my brother's house." She holds up her finger. "And two, I'm tired of living without you. I'm tired of telling myself that I'm not in love with you when I am." All I can do is look at her. This woman who pushes me to the edge of the cliff and makes me want to jump off. The woman who I will love for the rest of my life, regardless if I'm with her or not. "These past couple of weeks have shown me that, well, I'm a dumbass, and that I've put you through all of this for nothing. I know it's a lot to take in, and I really hope you can forgive me. So…" She points behind her. "I'm going to leave to give you your space and wait for you to think about what you need to think about."

Twenty-Six

Presley

"These past couple of weeks have shown me that, well, I'm a dumbass." I mean, I might as well call myself it especially since my mother pointed it out. "And that I've put you through all of this for nothing and I know that it's a lot to take in, and I really hope that you can forgive me. So…" I'm so nervous, and my heart is beating so fucking fast I can't focus on anything. The words just pour out of me. While I was sitting outside waiting for him, I promised myself that if he gave me even a minute, I would tell him everything. I just prayed that it wouldn't be too late. I just prayed that I haven't lost him forever. "I'm going to leave to give you your space and wait for you to think about what you need to think about." I turn and start walking to the door, every single step my feet feel as if they get heavier and heavier, and the last thing I want to do is walk out this fucking door. But I know that I just threw so many things at him at once, and he needs time to process it. I'm almost at the front door when I hear his throat clear, and I stop, hoping that he will tell me that it's not too late. Hoping that I didn't push him away for good. Knowing that if I did lose him, I have no one else to blame but myself.

"Um," he says, and I close my eyes for a second before I turn around to look at him. At this point, I'm not even trying to wipe away the tears because it's a lost cause. He stands there in the hallway, and I don't think I've ever wanted to hug him more in my life than I do right now. "That is a lot of things to take in."

I nod my head, trying to swallow but my mouth is so dry, and the lump in my throat grows bigger and bigger as time goes on. "It was a 'go big or go home' situation." I try to smile, but the tears just come, and I can feel my lower lip tremble. "Clarabella and Shelby said that it was do or die. Especially since you were dating." My eyes don't meet his, *and I want you to date me.*

He shakes his head and chuckles. "Your sisters are very aware that I'm not dating," he tells me, and I look at him shocked. "You don't think they came up to me yesterday to rip me a new asshole?" All that I can think is that I'm going to kill them when I speak to them again. Never during the whole time I poured out my heart to them did they tell me this. Not once. "These past couple of weeks I can't even put into words how it's been. I went from angry to hurt and back to angry again. But most of all, I missed you." He takes a deep inhale. "I'm not going back to how things were." The burning starts again in my stomach. "I don't want to never go out with you. I don't want you sneaking out of the house in the morning." I try not to get my hopes up as he takes a couple of steps toward me.

"What if we did date night three times a week?" I counter, taking a step closer to him, hoping to cut the distance between us. "Wherever or whenever you want." I take another step forward, hoping he doesn't back away. "And I promise to never, ever sneak out of the house in the morning." I don't tell him that what I want is for us to be in one house. That after being away from him these past couple of weeks, all I want is to be with him. "I want it all, and I want it with you."

He takes a step toward me. "It's been twelve years," he points out.

"I know," I say. "Trust me, I know. I spent all night going through it over and over."

"All night?" he asks as he takes one more step toward me, the distance getting shorter and shorter.

I can feel my heart start to beat so fast it might come out of my chest. "Since we are being honest." I tap my legs with my fingers to calm myself. "It wasn't just yesterday." I take one more step, and now we are almost face-to-face. "It's been from the beginning. I just didn't want to admit it to myself." I look down, and the need to touch him is so strong, but I hold it back. "I'm scared." I say those two words that I've never said in my whole life. Two words that make me feel the most vulnerable.

He puts his forefinger under my chin and lifts my head to look into his eyes. "You don't ever have to be scared when you are with me." His voice comes out in a whisper.

I raise my hands and place them on his chest. I can feel the heat coming through his shirt. I can feel the way his heart beats under my hand. "I promise that if you give me another chance, I will make it worth it." I lick my lips. "I'm sorry." I smile as the tears roll down. "I'm so sorry."

He puts his forehead on mine. "It's about fucking time," he says right before he softly kisses my lips. My hands move from his chest to his cheeks. "You aren't a dumbass." His hand falls from under my chin toward my hips. "But you are a pain in my ass." I throw my head back, and I can't help the laughter that escapes me. At that moment, I feel another kick, and I gasp. My hand goes to my stomach.

"It seems *our* baby"—I smile at him—"agrees with you." I take his hand and put it on my stomach, and now it's his turn to gasp.

"You got so big," he says, his eyes going big when the smile leaves my face. "I didn't mean it like that." I look down and see his hand on my stomach.

"It's not the only thing that got bigger," I mention to him, and my nipples tingle. "Also, I don't know what is in this baby thing, but I've never been hornier in my life."

"Is that your way of saying you missed my dick?" he

jokes with me, and I cup his cock.

"You know what I missed the most?" I ask him as my hand rubs up and down his cock. "Having this in my mouth." I don't even wait for him to say anything before I sink to my knees, my hands working in a frenzy to free his cock. It takes me less than a second, and the minute I pull his boxers down, his cock springs free. "Hi." My hand fists his cock as I lick the precum off him. "I missed you, too." I suck the head into my mouth, twirling my tongue around the head of his cock before taking half of it into my mouth again. "Hmm," I say, closing my eyes and trying to take him deeper and deeper.

"Gorgeous." He says my nickname, and all I can do is open my eyes and look up at him as I swallow his cock. His hips move just a touch to feed me more of his cock. My hand grips the base of his cock, jerking him. "Shit," he says and then takes a step back.

"What are you doing?" I ask him under protest when he lifts me.

"I haven't had you in a long time." His lips crash on mine, his tongue sliding against mine. "And the last place I'm going to come is in your mouth." He wraps his arm around my waist and picks me up.

"Well, at least I know eventually tonight you are coming down my throat," I tease as he walks up the stairs and to his bed. "We could fuck on the couch," I plead with him.

"I want you naked," he states, walking into his room. "In the middle of my bed." He puts me down, and his hand goes straight to the string behind my back. He pulls it loose, and the top falls down to my waist. "Fuck," he says, looking at my tits that are busting out of this half lace bra; he cups both tits, and I hiss out.

"They are so sensitive," I tell him, and he pushes it down, and my tits spring free.

"How sensitive?" he asks, bending and taking a nipple into his mouth. Sucking it deep and then biting while his hand twists the other nipple. "Does this make you…" He moves to the other nipple. "Wet?"

I rub my knees together. "No," I reply, my eyes closing as I roll my head back. "It makes me soaked." It comes out in a pant. "Dripping."

"Only one way to find out," he says, and he slips the dress over my hips, and it falls to my feet. He turns his hand around and slides his hand down my panties. His finger slides in, and he groans out now. My hand finds his cock as I jerk him off. "I'm going to fuck your tits after."

"You can fuck anything you want," I tell him as he slips another finger inside me. "As long as you fuck my pussy first."

"That sounds like a plan," he confirms as he takes his fingers out of me, and I groan out in protest. "But first, I'm going to eat it." He bites my lower lip. "I'm going to eat you as I've dreamed about eating you this whole time." He rips my panties from my hips and puts me in the middle of the bed. "Spread your legs," he orders me, and he doesn't have to tell me twice. He gets on his knees in the middle of my legs. His thumb comes down, and he makes a small circle over my clit. "You like that?" he asks, and I can't answer him because I'm panting with need. "You like this?" He does the circle again. "Or this?" He rubs the head of his cock up my slit and then sinks into me inch by fucking inch. "Fucking tight," he says as his balls hit my ass. I can't help bringing my knees up and getting him deeper. "Which one do you like?" he asks.

"Your cock," I say, trying to move my hips.

He takes his cock out and slides back in again. This time, both of us moan at the same time. "Now, do you like this?" He slams into me finally, and I can't help but roll my eyes to the back of my head. "Or this?" He pulls out his cock, and by the time I look down, his mouth is covering my pussy.

"Fuck, fuck," I chant as he sucks my clit into his mouth and then licks down to slide his tongue into me.

"So, cock?" He gets up and slides his cock into me, and then pulls out, and his tongue takes the place of his cock. "Or mouth?"

"Cock," I say, arching my back, and my hands move up to my tits as I pinch my own nipples and roll them.

"Okay, cock." He slides his cock into me, and his balls slap my ass. He fucks me slowly four times before he pulls his cock out of me. "Or finger?" He slides his two fingers into my pussy and fucks me.

"Bennett!" I scream out his name when I'm about to come, and he pulls his fingers out of me. "Why?" I moan. "Why?"

He takes his cock in his hand and slaps it right on my clit. "Because I want my cock in you when you come."

He slams into me. "Tell me how you want it."

"Fast and hard." I don't even have to think about it. "For round one." His eyes find mine, and then I look down and see his cock swallowed up by my pussy. "Round two has to be me riding you." One of my hands moves down to my clit. "Round three is with your tongue." My finger goes around in circles at my clit. "Round four is me in the kitchen bending over." I close my eyes as his cock rubs my G-spot over and over again. Sex with Bennett has always been out of this world, but with all these hormones in my body, this one is going to be one that we always talk about. "Then I want you to tit-fuck me and come in my mouth." His pace goes faster as his eyes watch his own cock. "I'm there," I tell him, and he just looks at me. "Right there," I say, and finally, I come all over his cock, my pussy pulsing over and over again and again.

He doesn't stop his pace. Instead, he picks it up, and when I finish coming, he slams into me twice more, and I'm coming again. "There she is," he says. "You're squeezing my cock so hard," he says between clenched teeth. "I'm going to come."

"My mouth." I say two words as I finish coming on his cock, and he slides out of me. I sit up, and the minute my mouth covers his cock, he places his hand on each side of my head as he fucks my face, and he comes down my throat with my name on his lips.

Twenty-Seven

Bennett

I feel her wiggle her ass on my cock in front of me, and then I'm pushed to my back. I feel like I just closed my eyes, and I have to wonder how long it's been since the last round. I'm about to say something when she grips my cock, and the only thing I can do is groan.

My eyes open at the exact time that she slides her pussy down my cock. My hands go to her hips. "Morning," I mumble as my hands come up, and I roll her nipples between my thumb and forefinger. She just moves up and down faster. We've been going at it the whole night. The whole fucking night, and neither of us is ready to give up.

She puts her hands on my chest and goes up and down

faster and faster, rotating her hips every single time she goes down. "I'm close," she says, and I want to laugh. She's been close all night long. I've lost count of the number of times she's come. "Bennett," she moans out my name, and I sit up with her, and my cock must go deeper in her. I wrap my arm around her waist and then flip her onto her back, my cock never coming out of her.

She wraps her legs around my waist. "This what you want?" I ask as I pound into her a couple more times before we both come at the same time. I collapse to the side and take her with me. "I need to sleep," I say, closing my eyes.

"You sleep, and I'm going to go and get something to eat," she replies, moving away from me and bending down to grab her robe. "I'll be back," she says, walking out of the room, and instead of lying in bed, I huff and get up, not about to let her go anywhere without me.

Putting on a pair of shorts, I walk downstairs and see her standing at the counter eating a cookie. "Can you go and get something in my car?" She looks over at me, and I see that it's just after seven in the morning.

"Sure," I say. "What am I getting?"

"My bag?" She grabs another cookie while she walks to the fridge. "I forgot to bring apple juice," she huffs. "We need to add that to the list."

I just nod at her and try to hide my smile with that last statement. It takes me less than three seconds to grab her bag and walk back in. "Did you pack apple juice?" I ask as I put the bag on the island.

"No." She looks up, and I can see that she has little

red spots all over her neck from my beard. "But I should have."

"So what's in the bag?" I laugh, walking over and kissing her neck.

"Some clothes and my toiletries," she says, and I stop in my tracks.

"Your clothes for today?" I look over at her.

"Not really. I just brought over a few things to keep here," she says, and after telling me she loved me, this is the best thing I've ever heard.

"Is that a fact?" I grab a bottle of water and lean on the counter to face her.

"Well, I wasn't going to count my chickens before they hatched, but I was hopeful that you would forgive me." She walks over to the bag and grabs it. "I'm going to be dragging my ass today."

"So, play hooky with me?" I suggest, knowing full well she will never do it. Even though I've asked her before, she won't.

"I guess I can." She walks over and grabs her phone while I just watch her. She presses buttons on her phone, and then I hear the sound of ringing.

"She fucking lives." I hear Clarabella's voice, and then she sits at the island and puts the phone down in front of her.

"Jesus Christ, it took you long enough." I hear Shelby's voice cut in. "We've been waiting all night."

"I've been busy." She smiles and then looks at me.

"I bet you have," Clarabella says. "Does that mean he didn't tell you to fuck off?"

"Of course, he didn't tell her to fuck off," Shelby retorts. "I was rooting for you the whole time." I shake my head and walk over to Presley and stand behind her. Looking at her phone and seeing Clarabella on the top and Shelby on the bottom of the FaceTime.

"She's a damn liar," Clarabella declares. "She bet me twenty bucks you wouldn't say yes until today." Shelby gasps out loud.

"Well, lucky for me," Presley says, reaching her arm out to wrap around my waist and pull me to her. "He said he didn't hate me." She looks up at me, and I'm still stunned that she is showing affection in front of her sisters. In the twelve years we've been with each other, she never showed anything to anyone. "Also"—she turns back to the camera—"you are both dead to me." She uses her thumbs to go across her neck as if she is cutting her throat. I can't help but put my hand on my forehead and laugh silently. I mean, I've known them my whole life, and I want to say that they weren't always crazy, but I'd be lying.

"For what?" Clarabella gasps.

"You guys knew Clarissa wasn't his date," she hisses at the screen. Clarabella starts looking up at the ceiling and not bothering to look at her.

"In our defense," Shelby says, "you never asked."

"I had a nervous breakdown in Mom's kitchen about it," Presley shares, and I whip my head to look at her.

"Oh my God, can we be more dramatic about this?" Shelby rolls her eyes. "You were having a nervous breakdown because he told you he loved you, and you were a dumbass. It had nothing to do with Clarissa."

"That is not true." She slaps the counter.

"Your man is standing there naked for all I know, and all you want to talk about is having a nervous breakdown," Clarabella chides. "You're my only brother-in-law that I haven't seen naked." She now laughs out loud.

"I've seen him naked," Shelby informs us.

"Excuse me?" Presley and I both gawk out.

"Relax, you two; it was when he was sixteen, and Travis dared him to go skinny-dipping." She rolls her eyes. "I saw one dingleberry and half of the twig." Shelby smiles.

"It's not a twig." I puff out my chest and fold my arms over my chest. "Tell her." I look over at Presley, who rolls her lips at me, trying not to laugh. "I'm waiting."

"I mean, not that I want to see it, but if I'm going to put my opinion out there, I have to see it." Clarabella shrugs.

"Absolutely not," Presley says. "Anyway, I'm calling to let you know I'm not going to be in today." Both her sisters look at her with shock. "We were up all night, and Bennett has the day off." She looks at me. "I'll see you both tomorrow."

"I'm off tomorrow also," I mumble.

"I'll see you guys in two days." She waves at the phone. "Byee," she sings out and gets up and winces. "What are the chances that we can take a nap?"

"You're staying home from work today and tomorrow?" I ask, not sure I actually heard her. I'm not saying that her job is her life, but I'm also not not saying it. It's one of the things I love most about her.

"If that is okay with you." She starts to grab the bag, and I put my hand on it to stop her from lifting it.

"It's more than okay with me," I assure her with a smile. "Now let's go take a nap."

"Like a real nap?" She tilts her head to the side. "Or like a *whoops, I didn't mean to shove my dick in your pussy* kind of nap?"

I can't help but laugh, and she slips her hand in mine as we walk up the stairs. "Hey, I have a question," she says as we walk into the room, and I put the bag on the bench in front of the bed. "What's your number?" I look over at her. "Like, how many women have you slept with?"

"Um…" I put my hands on my hips, not sure I want to answer this.

"I mean, I know you were with other people before me," she says. "But how many, you know, since me?" She holds up her hands. "Like, I know we weren't exclusive."

"Are you trying to tell me that you've been with other men?" The words taste like acid in my mouth.

"No." She laughs. "I've only ever been with you. I was wondering how many have you been with after me."

"Zero," I say, walking to her. "From the minute we kissed, it's only been you." I push the hair away from her face and kiss her lips softly. "Even with the back and forth while you were in college and then coming home here and there."

She smiles up at me as she wraps her arms around my

neck. "That's the sexiest thing you've ever said to me." She kisses under my chin. "Now let's get naked and go take a nap."

I chuckle. "Getting naked is going to have the opposite effect of us napping," I point out.

"No, it's not." She steps out of my hands and slips off the robe. "I think I'm going to go take a shower before a nap and wash off all that sex." She grabs the bag, and my eyes roam over her body. Her tits have always been fucking perfect, but now they are so full, and then my eyes go down to her small baby bump. "What are you looking at?" She looks at me sideways before unzipping the bag and grabbing her toiletry bag.

"How gorgeous you are." I smile slyly at her. "How sexy you are." She shakes her head and laughs. "And also how I didn't get to fuck your tits." That sends her over the edge, and now the room is filled with the sound of her laughter.

"Well, if you come with me in the shower, we can do that, and then when we come back to bed, we can really, really nap." She walks away from me to the bathroom, and I watch her ass.

"If you are going to twist my arm." I pull down my shorts and follow her into the bathroom. It takes us forty-five minutes in the shower, but that's only because after I fucked her tits, she sat down on the bench and played with herself, which then led to me getting on my knees.

"I'm getting out first." She kisses my chest. "And you have to wait five minutes because if I bend over, you're going to think I want you to have sex with me." I roll my eyes because one, she's not wrong, and two, I think I can control myself. "And I love you, but I really, really have to nap."

"Say it again." I pull her to me.

"Say what again?" She puts her head back and looks at me.

"Say you love me again." I bend to kiss her lips softly.

"I love you," she says, and my heart skips a fucking beat. This woman who drives me mad and pushes all my buttons owns every single piece of me. She gets on her tippy-toes and kisses the corner of my lips softly. "I love you." She kisses the other side of my lips. "I love you." Then she rubs her nose with mine. "I love you."

"I love you more," I tell her as I open the shower door for her, and she steps out, grabbing one of the white towels hanging. I watch her move around the bathroom, and I step out, grabbing my own white towel. She puts on one of my white T-shirts and walks out of the bathroom, and when I look over at the counter, I see her stuff mixed with mine. Her hairbrush is on the counter. Her face stuff is right next to my aftershave. It's my stuff with her stuff, and it might not seem like a big deal to anyone, but to me, it's everything.

I walk out and see that the bag on the bench in front of the bed is now tucked away in the corner under the chair. "There was a drawer that was empty," she says, coming out of the walk-in closet. "I put my things in there." She walks over to the bed and slides under the covers. "I hope it's okay."

I laugh, not saying anything as I walk into the closet

to grab a pair of boxers, and there it is, her stuff hanging next to mine. "It's more than okay," I mumble and walk back out without my boxers on. It takes us an extra thirty minutes before we really take a nap.

Twenty-Eight

Presley

The sound of the clicking of my heels fills the parking lot as I make my way up the steps toward the front door. The minute I pull it open, I feel the cold air fly out. "It's hotter than balls out there," I say, taking off my sunglasses.

"Well, considering someone has been balls deep inside you for the last two days." Clarabella snickers from behind the reception desk. "You should know."

I roll my eyes and try not to laugh at her stupid joke. "You trying to tell me no one was balls deep inside you?"

"We don't have sex every night." She rolls her eyes, and I know she's lying.

"Well, well, well." Shelby comes out of the kitchen

with a coffee cup in her hand. "Look what the cat dragged in." I laugh at her because for the past two days, we've been hunkered down in Bennett's house, neither of us wanting to step out of our cocoon. But today, he had to run into the office, and I figured I would come in.

"This dress cost two hundred dollars." I look down at the light pink, flowered one-piece dress I'm wearing. Every single pair of my pants got too tight for me, so I've been in dresses. "So there is no one dragging anyone."

"If he's not dragging you." Clarabella gets up and walks around the desk. "He's not doing it right."

"Are we going to discuss anything else but sex?" I walk toward my office, and both my sisters speak at the same time.

"No." I can't help but laugh.

"Well, I'm not discussing the sex, but I will say that I feel so liberated." I put my purse down in the chair and walk over to the desk.

"Oh, God, if she starts singing 'I am woman, hear me roar.'" Clarabella sits on the couch facing me. "I'm going home."

"I am not going to sing anything." I roll my eyes at her.

"So why do you feel so liberated?" Shelby asks as she sits next to Clarabella, who leans over and grabs her coffee cup to take a sip.

"I have no idea." I shrug. "Maybe because I'm not keeping the secret that I'm in love anymore."

"It wasn't a secret," Clarabella says. "And if it was a secret, you suck at keeping secrets." All I can do is glare at her. "Do you guys not have anything else to do today?"

"No, actually," Shelby says, grabbing her coffee cup back from Clarabella. "It's been a quiet week. We don't even have any scheduled appointments."

"Great," I say, clapping my hands and grabbing the phone. I dial the number and wait for the man to answer. "How is my favorite brother-in-law?" I look over at my sisters, who just look at me, wondering which one I'm talking to.

Luke laughs. "Yeah, right. What can I do for you?"

"Would it be possible to order lunch for two?" I ask him.

"Hey, baby!" Clarabella yells from the couch, and Luke laughs even harder.

"Is the lunch for my woman?" he says, and I put my finger in my mouth and fake vomit.

"It's for your woman's pregnant sister and her man," I say and look over at my sisters, seeing them shake their heads and laugh.

"I'll fix something up," he huffs. "Come by at eleven." I look at my watch and see that it's just after nine. "Tell my woman if she joins you, I'll give her something special."

"Eww," I say and hang up while he laughs. "He said if you go there, he'll give you something special." She smirks at me.

"Where are you taking lunch?" Shelby asks, and I smile at her.

"I thought I would surprise Bennett and take him on a

picnic." I watch my sisters' faces in shock.

"Whatever you do," Shelby says, "leave your phone in the car." She closes her eyes, and I can't help but laugh. A while ago, she had a picnic with Ace, and well, one thing led to another, and by accident, she butt-dialed us in the middle of her adventure. Needless to say, there was enough panting and moaning for us to get the gist of it.

"I still have that voice mail saved," Clarabella says, and Shelby hits her. "It's called leverage."

"Okay, you two, I need for you to get out so I can do all my work for the week in two hours." I shoo them with my hands. I leave a little bit after eleven, and when I walk into the restaurant, I see Luke behind the bar.

"My favorite sister-in-law." He laughs, and I take out my phone from my purse.

"Can you say that again while I film you?" I ask him, laughing, and he walks around the bar grabbing the picnic basket from one of the stools.

"Here you go." He hands me the basket. "Everything is in there."

"Look at how pretty this is," I say, holding it up and checking it out. "It's very *Wizard of Oz*," I say of the brown wicker basket.

"It's Shelby's. She got it when she had that picnic with Ace." He rolls his lips when my smile turns to disdain.

"Eww." I cringe. "They probably had sex on top of this."

Luke throws his head back and laughs. "And let's hope she's the only one," he teases. "Also, I don't want it back." Now it's my turn to laugh as I wave goodbye to him and walk out of the restaurant. I make my way over to Bennett's office, and when I park my car, my stomach starts to flutter as I pull open the door. I've never just shown up at his office in the middle of the day, let alone to take him out to lunch. My feet move before I chicken out and get back into my car.

My palms get sweaty as I smile at the receptionist and ask to see Bennett. *Maybe I should have called before I came in*, I think to myself. My stomach feels like it's going to throw up when I hear shoes coming toward the area. He smiles big when he sees me, and all the nerves I had before are gone. He's wearing dark blue dress pants with a white button-down shirt with the collar open. His hair looks like he just ran his fingers through it, and his eyes light up. He's everything. "Well, this is a surprise," he says to me, and I take two steps to him and kiss his lips, surprising him. I've never, ever kissed him in public before. I mean, minus a couple of drunk kisses in the bar or at the car when he was driving me home.

But out in the open? Never. "I thought we could have lunch together," I say softly. "I mean, if you aren't too busy."

The smile on his face says it all. "Well, isn't this a coincidence since I'm free."

My face fills with the same smile that is on his face now. "Well, isn't this my lucky day," I say to him.

"Come on back while I close up a couple of things." He motions with his head as we walk down the hallway. My hand itches to hold his, but by the time I've talked myself into holding his, we are in his office.

"Where is Andrew?" I point at the desk out in the empty hallway.

"He's off for the week," Bennett says, grabbing a couple of folders. "We all are. I just had to come in and sign a couple of things."

"Well, now isn't that a coincidence." I tilt my head to the side. "I'm off also."

He comes to stand in front of me, and I look up at him. "I wonder what we can do with our time off." He tilts his head to the side.

"I hear naked Sunday is really fun," I joke with him as we walk out of his office, and my hand slides into his. His eyes go down to our hands. "Is this okay?" The burning in my neck starts, and I think that maybe we should have talked about this before I just went and held his hand. "It's fine." I smile as I take my hand out of his. But he's quick to grab my hand back, and his fingers slip between mine. "We don't have to hold hands."

"You're right, we don't," he says, pushing open the door to outside, "but I want to." He picks our joined hands up and kisses my fingers. "Now, are we taking your car or mine?"

"We should take mine since the food is in there." I point at my car, and he stops walking.

"You picked up food already?" he asks, surprised.

"Well, yeah, I thought it would be nice to have a picnic." I shrug. "It's okay if you don't want to eat the food. We can go anywhere."

"A picnic sounds nice," he murmurs softly, stopping

and grabbing my face in his hands. "Now give me the keys," he says right before he bends to kiss my lips. "I like when you surprise me at work."

I throw my head back and laugh at him, grabbing my keys from my purse. "This is the only time I've surprised you at work."

"I know." He grabs the keys and walks around the car with me, opening the passenger door for me. "And I like it." He slams the door and walks around to the driver's side. He gets in, starting the car, and then adjusting the seat. "So where to?" he asks as he puts on his seat belt.

I give him the directions to a little spot that I found when I was doing a tour with another bride. It's very secluded and right next to a stream. The heavy, dense trees block most of the sun, making it cool. He grabs the basket of food while I grab the bag with the blanket and pillows. He slides his hand into mine as I navigate through the grass toward the secret passage. "Isn't this pretty?" I ask him as we stop.

"I've lived here my whole life, and I've never been here," he says, and I smile big, grabbing the blanket and placing it on the ground. I kick off my heels, then toss the pillows on the blanket. "It's so peaceful." He kicks off his own shoes while unbuttoning the cuff at his wrist and rolling up the first sleeve and then the next. He sits on the blanket and leans over to kiss me.

"So I have to know." I get up on my knees and go over to the food basket. "Good surprise, or don't-do-it-again surprise?" Opening the basket, I check out the different types of sandwiches that Luke made.

He laughs at me, grabbing me by the hips and pulling me to him. I straddle his legs, sitting on him. "This is the best surprise," he assures me, pushing my hair back to see my face. "I mean, not the best surprise." I gasp. "I think the best surprise was waking up with you riding me." I roll my eyes. "Or with my dick in your mouth." He rolls his lips. "No, actually, the best surprise was you telling me you love me." He kisses my lips. "But this is high up there."

I put my hands on his chest. "I was way out of my comfort zone." I swallow. "And to be honest, I almost ran out of the office while I was waiting for you."

"Thank you." He kisses me softly. "For doing this."

"You're welcome." I'm about to kiss him when I feel a little kick, and my mouth and eyes open. "The baby just kicked." I grab his hand and put it on my stomach, really hoping that he can feel it. "Why don't you kiss me again?" I tell him. "It usually gives me butterflies in my stomach."

"I give you butterflies." He smiles, his voice going soft.

"You always gave me butterflies," I admit to him, leaning in and kissing his lips softly. "It's like the first time all over again," I say, my lips on his through a smile, and then I feel the kick again and so does he.

"Oh my God." He gasps, looking down at his hand on my stomach. "I felt it." He places his other hand on top of mine. "I felt it." He moves his hands now and holds my hips, lifting me off him as he sets me next to him so he can bend his head and talk to my stomach. "Hey there, it's me, your dad." He places both hands on my stomach. "Sorry I haven't been around the past couple of weeks."

"It's your mom's fault," I cut in and tell the baby. "She's had her head up her a—" I'm about to say ass and then rethink it. "Her butt." I shrug. "But it's fine now."

"It's more than fine." He kisses my stomach. "Now, I'll get you and your mom fed." He looks over and grabs two sandwiches out of the basket. "Oh, there is apple juice."

"That's mine," I say, grabbing the juice from him. "He put a beer in there for you."

I unwrap one of the sandwiches and see that I got the turkey one. "What do you have?" I look over at him, and he unwraps a ham one. "I don't want that one," I say, shaking my head, and he laughs.

"Well, then, lucky for me, this is the one I wanted." He takes a bite as he grabs the brown bag, and when I look inside, I see that it's homemade chips. "Are you really off for the rest of the week?"

I nod my head, taking a bite of the sandwich. "What do you want to do?" I ask him, and he just shrugs while he chews.

"Don't care as long as you're there," he says, and I smile.

"If we are going to go back to your place, I'm going to need to stop and get some clothes from my house," I inform him, and my stomach forms knots when I think about what I really want to ask him.

"We can stay at your house also," he says, looking at me. "Whatever you want."

"What if I don't want to have two houses?" I ask him and take a bite of my sandwich before I just blurt out everything instead of going slow.

"What do you mean?" he asks me, and I look up at him.

"I mean, what if instead of having two houses"—I take a sip of the apple juice, putting the back of my hand against my forehead—"we have just one?" My hand starts to shake. "Forget it, it was a bad idea." I ignore the way my heart is pounding in my chest and put down the sandwich because right now, all I want to do is vomit.

"You don't know this," he says softly, and my eyes fly up to his as he puts his food down beside him. "But the night you ended up in the hospital, I was going to ask you to move in." My hand flies to my mouth. "I had all these flowers at the house, and I was going to make you dinner and well…"

"I would have said no." The words come out, and he just smirks at me. "And not because I didn't want to but because I was..."

"I know," he says. "Trust me, I know." His legs prop up, and he rests his forearms on them. "These past couple of days." He looks down and then looks up. "Have been everything." I smile because they really have been.

"It should have been like this all along." I wipe the tear that has escaped. "And I'll forever be sorry that I did that to us."

"It's our story," he says. "It's the way it had to be. I'm not going to lie." He chuckles. "I did expect to wake up and find you gone this morning." I smile sadly. "I'm really fucking happy you were in my arms."

"I'll be in them for as long as you want me there," I say, and he pulls me to him.

"Yes," he says, and I tilt my head. "Let's have one house." I can't help but smile, and the tears come even if I wanted them not to come. "The question is, which house?"

Twenty-Nine

Bennett

"Are you sure that you know what you're doing?" Clarabella looks at me, and I put my head back and groan.

"I'm pretty sure I know how to twist a tube," I tell her as she taps her pen on the pad in front of her. "Unless it's changed again."

"It has not been changed." She smirks. "We did have to shut down a couple of suggestions from Travis and my mother."

"Oh, God." I grab my cup of coffee and take a sip. "Do I want to know?"

"Travis thought it would be a great idea to put you in nets and for us to kick balls at you until one of them exploded pink or blue." She taps her finger. "That was a maybe."

"Absolutely not," I say, shaking my head.

"We would have given you equipment so you can have more babies." She smirks at me and then looks down at my junk.

"Gorgeous!" I yell for Presley, who comes out of the bedroom. It's been a month since we decided to move in together. I mean, it's been a month since she said we should have one home. It took two days while we were off to go to her house and grab everything that she wanted to bring over. It took two more days before I saw little pieces of her all over the house. The throw pillows on the couch. The pictures of us now scattered around the house. It was exactly what I pictured when I bought this house. It was a dream to me. Waking with her every single day and then coming home to her. It was like a switch was flipped in her, and she was all-in. She would call me during the day. She would show up with snacks just for fun to see me. Before I thought she cared for me, there is no mistaking that she loves me. Every single time she says goodbye, it's followed with an I love you.

"Yes, dear." She smiles as she walks down the stairs. She's wearing a tight one-piece dress that shows her little belly, her hair is pinned up, and her eyes are shining as she makes her way to me. "I'm here." She hugs my waist, and I put a hand around her shoulder and kiss her head.

"Look at how cute you look." Clarabella grins and claps her hands as she looks her up and down.

"Well, now that it doesn't look like I overate and it

actually looks like a baby bump, I might as well flaunt it." She rubs her belly. Just this morning, she got a little bit enraged that she felt fat. It took me fifteen minutes of talking her off the ledge. And by that, I mean I went and bought a cookie, which then made her smile.

"You don't even look pregnant from the back," Clarabella says, and Presley just glares at her.

"Why are you even here?" Presley asks her between clenched teeth.

"We have to go over the gender reveal details." Clarabella looks down at the pad in front of her. "We already went over decorations and the guest list." Clarabella puts a check. "And Bennett nixed Travis's idea." She puts an X next to it and looks up at me with her eyebrows raised.

"I already nixed that," Presley says. "Not going to happen." She lets go of me and walks over to the fridge and grabs the apple juice. "Neither is Mom's."

"Should I even ask what that was?" I ask, and Presley shakes her head.

"She wanted to do fireworks and then have a plane fly over you and throw colored water on us," Clarabella informs me, and I want to say that nothing surprises me with them, but that right there. That takes the cake.

"How about a pinata?" I ask.

"How about no." Clarabella doesn't even skip a beat.

"We are going to have the simple poppers." I hold up my hand. "That shoots out confetti." I look over at Presley.

"I want that." Presley points at me. "Nothing

extravagant."

Clarabella throws her head back and laughs. "Nothing extravagant, sure." She closes the book she was writing in. "Okay, whatever you say." She pushes away from the island. "And don't forget you have to wear pink or blue. Whatever you think the baby is." She walks out the door, slamming it behind her.

"Why can't we just find out and pick up the phone and call people like they did in the old days?" I ask Presley, who just shakes her head.

"That would be way too easy." She laughs. "Are you driving to the doctor or am I?"

I push off, putting the coffee cup in the sink. "You know what would really be funny," I say, grabbing her hand as we walk out of the house. "If she can't tell the sex of the baby, and we put in yellow confetti."

"Don't even put that in the universe, Bennett," Presley grits between clenched teeth. "Take it back." She glares at me, and all I can do is roll my lips to keep from laughing.

"Do you think maybe we should have found out the sex of the baby before everyone else?" Presley comes into the bathroom in a blush strapless lace bra with matching panties, and one look at her makes my cock rise. "Like, what if the poppers go off and we're upset?"

"Is that bra new?" I turn, wiping my hand on the hand towel.

"Don't you 'is that a new bra' with me and don't even think of ripping these panties." She folds her arms under her tits, making them even more plump.

"That's not helping." I walk to her. "We can always slide them to the side."

"Knock, knock, knock, knock." I hear the front door slam and tilt my head to look at her.

"It defeats the point when they yell knock, knock, knock, knock and they are already in the house." I bend and kiss her lips.

"You can try to keep them out," she whispers, "but nothing will help." Her eyes fly down to my dick. "You might want to put away your soldier before they come up."

"Why are they even here?" I hiss. "They told us to be there in twenty minutes. We aren't even late."

"Um, hello, are we ready to go?" Wwe hear being yelled from the staircase. "Can someone answer me, or I'm going to think that you guys are up there trying to get another baby in her."

"Can you imagine," Presley says. "Already this one is tight." She turns and walks out of the bathroom and toward the hallway. I slip on shorts and a T-shirt and look over to see her walk out in a sundress.

"Why do we need to get ready at the venue?" I ask and it's at that moment I know that I'm not asking one more question for the rest of the day. Even when we get there and they usher me into another room so she can get glammed up.

"How're you doing?" Travis asks me when he comes

into the room ten minutes after I got here. I'm sitting on the couch, watching television with a bucket of beer in front of me.

"This is the most ridiculous thing I've ever done," I admit when I do a circle with the remote in my hand. "They won't even let me see her." My eyes look up and down, and I see him wearing blue pants with a baby-pink jacket. "What the hell are you wearing?"

"I didn't want to pick sides, so I'm neutral," he says, and I slap my leg, laughing, knowing that this is not going to go over well.

"Did anyone see you?" He sits down, grabbing a beer.

"Nope, and I'm hiding until it's time." He shakes his head, taking a pull of the beer. "You ready?"

"Not even close," I tell him, and then we don't say another word until Shelby comes in the room.

She's wearing a baby-pink dress. "Okay, so we have ten minutes to get out there. People are already mingling."

I put my beer down on the table and get up. "Where is Presley?"

"She's getting into her dress," Shelby says. "So you need to get into your suit. I'm not going to say she's cranky, but I'm not not saying it." She turns and starts to walk out. "Next time you knock her up, I'm leaving for nine months."

I walk over to the baby-blue suit with a white button-down shirt, leaving the first two buttons open because I know she likes to kiss me near my collarbone. "If it helps," Travis says, "you look sexy as fuck." I can't stop the laughter that roars out of me.

We walk out of the room and head toward the party space. "Whoa," Travis says beside me. "This is…"

"What the fuck?" I mumble, seeing all the decorations. There are two high tables as soon as you walk in, one with a blue tablecloth, the other with a pink. Between the tables is a sign that says old wives' tales. Little details are telling you what she craves, how she sleeps, how high or low she is carrying. There is a huge wall full of pink, blue, and clear balloons around a sign that says *He or She?*

There are big pink and blue balloons all over the place with long tables in the middle of the room with white tablecloths and vases of pink, white, and blue flowers. "Hi," Clarabella says when she comes to me, and she's also wearing a pink dress, but hers is hot pink. "We are doing the poppers in about ten minutes."

"Where is Presley?" I ask, looking around, and I see her walking into the room, and my chest fills with even more love. Her black hair is loose, and she wears a strapless baby-pink dress. The top is tight until just under her boobs, and then it kicks out with what can only be described as thousands of layers of dress. It's so puffy, but it stops just above her knee in the front, but it falls to the floor in the back. I see her spin as she looks around, and it looks like every layer in the back has more and more tulle.

My feet walk on their own as I walk toward her. "You look…" I say when I get close enough, my arm going around her waist and being swallowed by the dress. "You've never looked more beautiful."

She smiles up at me, her eyes shining with happiness. "You don't look so bad yourself," she says right before I bend and kiss her lips. We don't have much alone time before we are pulled over to the side where there is a table filled with poppers.

"Okay, so we thought it would be better if we all pop one," Clarabella says. "The pictures will be amazing."

I stand by the table as Clarabella tells everybody how it's going to go down. "Are you nervous?" I bend down and whisper in her ear, and all she can do is smile, but I see tears in her eyes.

"I don't care what we are having as long as the baby is healthy." She blinks away the tears and fans her face.

"Now"—Clarabella hands us each a popper—"on the count of three." She looks around the room. "And this is being filmed, so if you go before, I'm going to know who it is." She moves her finger back and forth around the room.

"She's scaring our guests," I mumble and Presley just rolls her lips.

"Okay, people," Clarabella starts saying. "One."

"I love you," Presley says beside me.

"Two!" Clarabella shouts.

"I love you more," I declare, and when I hear three, I turn the bottom of the popper, and so does everyone else. The pink confetti fills the room, and all I can do is open my mouth in shock and happiness and look over at Presley, who has the same look on her face. She looks at the pink confetti falling on her, and it's at that moment that I take the next step.

I get down on one knee beside her, and the gasps fill the room, and she looks over at me. She puts her hands over her mouth, and she sobs out. "No," she says even before I ask anything, and everyone in the room goes quiet after she says that. "I was the one who had to propose." She shakes her head. "We had a plan." She points at her sisters, who nod, agreeing with her.

"Well, too bad," I say, looking over at Travis. "We had a plan also." Travis comes to stand beside me and hands me the box that I gave him before walking out.

"I can't believe you two," Shelby hisses.

"Why wouldn't you tell me?" Clarabella glares at Travis.

"Like you two told me?" Travis argues back.

"It was a surprise," Shelby snaps.

"Same," Travis retorts, and then Mrs. Baker snaps.

"I swear to God if this is on video and is being recorded, I'm going to hurt someone." She turns and looks at her kids, who all hold up their hands. Then she turns to me with a sweet smile. "Go on, dear."

"Presley," I begin, looking at her and seeing the tears run down her face. "Twelve years ago."

"Don't you dare," she says between clenched teeth, and she looks over at her mother, who glares at her. "I was eighteen, everyone. Relax."

"Like I was saying, twelve years ago, we went on our first date." I kind of lie just a bit to that. "I knew that it was special. I just didn't know how special it was." I grab her hand and bring it to my lips. "There is no one that I can picture beside me for the rest of my life but you. There is no one I want beside me for the rest of my life but you. You make me smile and frown, sometimes at the same time." The room laughs. "You drive me bonkers, but then you make it all better with just one smile." I smile through my own tears. "You've given me the ultimate gift by carrying our daughter." I choke when I say the words. "I would be honored and privileged to call you my wife. Will you marry me?"

"This isn't fair," she whines. "I had this whole speech, and now it's gone."

"Good," Mrs. Baker says. "Now answer his question."

"I want to counter your proposal," she says, laughing,

Travis groans, "Of course she does." He throws his hands in the air.

"I'll accept the proposal under one condition," she says, and I know that whatever she says, I'm going to give her because it's her. It's always been her. "We get married now."

"I'll accept the proposal under one condition." I look down at him, and I can't help but feel like I've got the whole world now. Like I'm literally floating on cloud nine, but I'm missing one thing to make it even more complete. Calling him my husband. "We get married now."

"You can't get married now." My mother puts her hand on her forehead. "You don't even have a dress."

"I can wear this one." I look down at the dress I'm wearing now. "I mean, it was a wedding dress. We just altered it."

"But it's pink," my mother says between clenched teeth.

"Mom, I don't think anyone is going to believe her if she walks down in a white dress." Clarabella leans in and tells her, "That ship has sailed."

"At least six months ago," Shelby adds in, and in return, my mother just bites down even harder on her teeth.

"I'm down," Bennett agrees. "Although I would like to change my suit."

"I second that," Shelby says. "You look like cotton candy."

"No, he doesn't." I look down at him. "You look handsome."

"Well, he can look even more handsome," Clarabella suggests, "in the black tux that I brought for him." We just look at her. "Please, this isn't our first rodeo."

"Okay, great," I say, clapping my hands. "Let's get me married."

"So is that a yes to marrying me?" Bennett asks, and I see he's still on one knee.

"Of course." I grab his face and bend down. "Yes, yes, yes," I say, kissing his lips. "Always yes." I smile, and I wipe the lip gloss off his lips. "I was supposed to propose to you."

"Over my dead body," he jokes, getting up now and kissing me. "Now, how fast can we get married?"

"Thirty minutes," Shelby says. "We have the venue in the other room already set up."

I look at her shocked. "Isn't that for the wedding we are having this weekend?"

"That's what we told you," Clarabella says. "Now are

we still one- hundred percent down with this dress?"

I look down at the dress and nod my head. "It's pretty and sassy." I look down. "It's me, and I love it." I smile at Bennett. "And I knew that when I put it on, it was what I wanted to get married in."

Twenty minutes later, my mother is walking me down the aisle where the wedding goes off without a hitch.

Three months later

"So what did the doctor say?" Clarabella asks me as I sit on the couch in my living room. I'm wearing a blue sundress because nothing else fits me at this point.

"It can happen at any minute," I huff. "I'm a week late at this point. She said that I can go up to fourteen days." I look down at the basketball of my stomach. "I'm going to be really, really mad if you stay in here another seven days." I rub my stomach. "She is exactly where she's supposed to be."

"Here you go." Bennett hands me the glass of apple juice, and I smile up at him. He bends and kisses my lips.

"Thank you," I say, and he picks up my feet from the couch and sits with them in his lap.

"But what did you guys decide?" Shelby comes over from the kitchen with a plate of fruit for herself as she offers me some. "Like, did you ask how many can be in the room?"

"She said it's the husband and a support person." I

repeat what the doctor said. "You guys can fight with Mom."

"Bennett," Clarabella calls out to him. "Do you really want to be in there?" I roll my lips when all he does is look at her like she's out of her mind. "I mean, you've already seen her vagina in detail. Do you want to see it with a human coming out of it?" I close my eyes now, not even willing to picture my own vagina the way she described it.

"I'm one thousand percent sure that I want to watch my child being born," he says, and I open my eyes when I feel wetness between my legs.

I move my legs off Bennett and stand. "I think I peed myself," I say, and my sisters' eyes fly to the middle of my legs.

"You think?" Clarabella sits up. "There is like water dripping down your leg."

"Oh my God." Shelby all but throws the plate of fruit. "It's happening."

"What's happening?" Bennett sits up and looks down. "It's leaking everywhere."

"It's her water," Clarabella says, running up the stairs. "I'll get the bag." She walks into our bedroom. "Why does it smell like coconut oil and sex in your room?"

"Eww," Shelby says. "Did you do anal?"

"What?" I shriek. "Why would you even ask that?"

"I've heard coconut oil helps make things easy," Shelby says, and I look over at Bennett, who is standing there in shock with his fist right in front of his mouth.

"I don't want to touch anything in this room,"

Clarabella declares, coming out. "I need to, I don't know, like bleach my whole body." She dumps my hospital bag by my feet. "Shit, the baby bag?" She runs up the stairs and stops. "Why the hell are you guys even having sex?" She holds the railing, looking at us.

"The doctor said it could help," Bennett says in his defense.

"You had sex this morning," Shelby accuses, and I look at her. "And then went to see the doctor with your vag full of sperm." She fake vomits. "What is wrong with you?" She looks from me to Bennett, who puts his hands on his head. "I'm telling Mom."

I'm about to say something to her when a sharp pain rips through me, and I scream, holding the couch. "What the fuck was that?" I pant out. "I'm dying." I put my hand on my stomach.

"Let's get you in the car." Bennett keeps calm while Shelby grabs my bag, and Clarabella finally returns with the baby bag.

I take a couple of steps before I have to stop again. "Aggggghhhh," I groan, grabbing my stomach. "I'm sorry, but this is not what it said in the book." I look at Bennett, who is just trying to get me into the car. He holds my elbow as he walks with me. "That felt like someone stabbed me with a knife."

"We will get you to the hospital," Bennett assures me as we all pile in the car.

"Someone is going to have to time the contractions," Bennett orders as he pulls out of the driveway.

"On it," Shelby says, taking out her phone. "Just let

me know."

I look over at her, and another one comes. "Now," I say right before more water pours out of me. "Oh my God." I look down. "It's like I'm sitting in a puddle of water."

The window in the back is pulled down, and Clarabella sticks her head out. "I'm going to be sick." The wind blows her hair back. "You need to sell the car. Who is going to sit in her vagina juice?"

"Oh my God," I say, looking down. "How much water is in me?" I look at Bennett, who, at this point, has turned a pale white. "Here comes another one." I start my breathing. "That wasn't so bad." I look back at Shelby. "How much time between?"

"What?" she asks and looks down at the phone in her hand. "I forgot to press the button."

"Oh my God!" I yell out.

"It's not my fault." Shelby starts puffing out. "I have her in the back with her head sticking out of the car like a dog. I have you in the front leaking I don't even know what." She puts her hand to her head. "I think I'm going to faint."

"It doesn't matter. We are here now," Bennett states as he pulls into the parking lot at the hospital. He parks the car. "Fuck," he says, looking at me. "I didn't call the doctor."

"Well, I'm sure someone will call her," Shelby says, opening the door and grabbing the bags.

Clarabella gets out of the car and opens the door for me. "Let me help you." She holds out her hand, and I grab it, putting one foot out and then the other. I stand and drip all over. Clarabella looks down at the water on her feet. "It's fine," she says. "It's not fine. It's not fine." She lets go of my hand. "I don't volunteer as tribute." She shakes her head. "I don't even want to be in there. I'm out."

"Oh, would you stop it." Shelby pushes her to the side and hands her the bag. "Can we get her inside?"

But Bennett has me by the hand, and we are already walking inside. "Of all days for your water to break, you think it's a good idea to do it with your sisters here," he mumbles as he presses the button to the elevator.

"You think I planned this?" I look at him. "This is not like it was supposed to go," I remind him, right before the biggest contraction of my life runs through me. I literally have to bend over. "Oh my God," I pant as I get into the elevator with my sisters.

"What floor?" Shelby asks me, and I just look at her. "Oh, for the love of God," she hisses and steps out of the elevator, stopping the first person she sees. "Maternity?"

"Eighth floor," the man says, and Shelby turns, rushing back into the elevator and pressing eight five million times.

"Thank God you pressed it that many times. It makes the elevator go faster," Clarabella deadpans and looks at me. "She's leaking all over the elevator." She turns and puts her forehead against the wall of the elevator. "Should I press the emergency button and be like *cleanup on aisle eight*?" she mimics, and if I wasn't in so much pain, I might even laugh.

The elevator doors open, and I waddle out, walking to the desk. "Hi," Bennett says. "My wife is having a baby."

"Obviously, she's having a baby. Why else would you be here?" Shelby says.

"She's leaking everywhere," Clarabella points out. "Like, she must have zero water left inside her."

The nurse looks at all of us, and I try to say something, but all I can do is hold the desk in front of me. "She's in active labor."

"She's doing something," Clarabella says. "We tried timing stuff but..."

"Right this way," the nurse says, and I try to follow her, but I have to stop, and she runs to get a wheelchair.

"You should put a towel on that," Clarabella urges, but I just sit, and it hurts my butt.

"I feel pressure," I tell the nurse who rushes into the room.

"What else do you feel?" she asks. "Please get into the bed."

"I feel like someone is trying to get out of my vagina," I tell her. "Like, literally crawl out of me like a Transformer."

"Oh, good God," Bennett says as he helps me get into the bed, but a pain rips through me, and all I can do is put my elbows on the bed as I rock from side to side.

"When did this all start?" she asks, and I look at my sisters.

"I don't know," Shelby says. "We were sitting down. They had just come home from the doctor."

"Did she tear your membranes?" the nurse asks me, and I just stare at her. "Okay, let's see what's going on," she says, and I open my legs.

"Is that blood?" Bennett asks as I try to look down there, but with my stomach, I can't see shit. He comes over to my side and holds my hand. "It's okay."

"What is it?" I look at Shelby, who has her hands on her cheeks. "Is it bad?"

"Could be the mucus plug," the nurse explains.

"I'm never, ever having a child," Clarabella declares as she puts a hand to her mouth. "I can't do it."

The nurse cuts off my panties, and she gasps. "Oh, my, she's crowning," she says, and I have no idea what that means. She springs up and runs over to the monitor. "We have a crowning in room seven," the nurse says, looking at me. "We need a heated bed and a doctor STAT."

"What can we do to help?" Shelby asks, looking around.

"Go keep mom calm," the nurse says, motioning to me with her chin. "Whatever you do, don't push."

"Don't push?" I yell out. "I need drugs." I look at her. "It's in my birth plan. I'm not doing this without drugs."

"Oh, we are way past that," she announces, and she runs out of the room.

"I have a couple of Xanax," Clarabella says, going for her purse. "If you chew them, they might kick in, and you'll be asleep before you remember any of this."

"Okay, people." A man comes in clapping his hands, followed by four other people with a bed, and I don't even know what.

"Cover her," Shelby tells Bennett.

"He's the doctor," Bennett says. "He's going to see a lot more than that."

"Okay, we need to get her undressed," the nurse says.

"Just cut it off," Clarabella says, and I just stare at her. "Like, you are never going to wear this dress again. It's got bodily fluid on it and mucus and all that stuff."

I'm about to yell at her when a sharp pain comes. "Oh my God!" I yell when the burning fills my vagina. It's like a pot of hot water is being thrown up in my vagina. "It burns."

"What is that?" Clarabella asks, standing next to the doctor looking straight at my vagina. "Why is it red?" She looks at me. "Why is it so puffy?"

"Okay, so we are going to start to push the next time a contraction comes," the doctor explains. "We are all going to count to ten." I feel the pain coming, the tightness starts right away, and I groan. "Okay, and push," the doctor says, and I push as they count.

"Oh my God, the head is coming," Clarabella says, leaning next to the doctor's head and all he can do is smile at her. "It's a girl," she informs him, and I don't have any time to say anything while another one starts to come.

"Okay, I want you to push like you have to take a big poop," the nurse tells me. "And go."

"You can do this," Bennett soothes from beside me, kissing my forehead.

"I didn't think your vagina could get bigger," Clarabella says. "I was wrong."

"Damn," Shelby says when she looks down, and Bennett is about to go and look, and I squeeze his hand.

"Don't you dare," I warn between clenched teeth.

"Don't do it, bro," Clarabella agrees. "You'll never look at it the same." She shakes her head and looks away.

"Push," the doctor says, and I push with everything that I have. My eyes close as I hear them count.

"Oh my God, the whole head is out," Clarabella says, and she puts her hand on her head. "It's like a human head is coming out of her."

"Don't push," the doctor says, and I don't have to guess what he's doing because Clarabella tells me.

"He's literally turning the baby's head," she says between clenched teeth. "Is that safe?" She looks at the doctor, who just laughs at her.

"This is the most fun I've ever had," the doctor says, laughing. "Okay, I think one more push, and we are going to have the shoulders out, and then it should be smooth sailing."

"I don't know if I can do that," I say, getting suddenly so tired. "It hurts."

"You got this," Bennett coaches, and I take a big breath in. "If anyone can do this, you can."

"You got this," Shelby encourages from beside me.

"I have faith in you," Clarabella says. "I mean, at this point, you're a hero."

The nurse puts a blanket on my stomach when I bear down, and when we get to seven, the doctor looks at me. "Here we go," he says, and I don't know what he means, but one second later, he's placing my baby on my stomach. "We have a baby," he says, but my arms are already around her as the sobs rip through me.

"My baby," I say, looking down at her with Bennett's head next to mine. "We have a baby," I tell him, and he's got his own tears running down his face. "Hi, honey," I say, kissing the baby as she blinks her eyes at us. "Welcome to the world, baby girl."

Epilogue Two

Bennett

Five years later

"Are you ready, my princess?" I put the apple juice back in the fridge and look over at my daughter, Violet, who is sitting at the island.

"I need my bow, Daddy," she says, turning and getting off her stool as she hops toward the couch where she left her hair tie. "You do it for me, Daddy?" She comes back and hands it to me.

"Um…" I look at the tie in my hand and at my daughter's black hair. "How about we ask Mommy to do it?"

"You can't do it?" Violet puts her hands on her hips

and tilts her hip. Her blue eyes just look at me. "Auntie Clarabella says girls run the world anyway." Violet shrugs at me. "It's okay, Daddy. You can cut the grass better than Mommy."

I don't even know what to say to her. "Thanks." I bend and pick her up. "For the vote of confidence," I say, grabbing my keys. "And just so you know, boys and girls run the world." I kiss her nose as I put her in her booster seat, and she pushes my hand away.

"I can do it myself," Violet tells me, and I just look at her. She is the stamp of her mother. There is no denying that she is her mini-me. But she is also the most independent kid I've ever met. She has to do everything herself, even if she can't do it, she will try to do it, and only when she gets to her wit's end will she look for help, but even then, it's like pulling teeth for her to ask for it. The other day, we were outside in the backyard, and she was trying to climb the monkey bars. Instead of asking me to hold her or spot her, she did it by herself. She fell over and over again but got up, and after four fucking hours, she crossed it. "Are we getting Starbucks for Mommy?"

"Not today." I get into the driver's seat and look in the rearview mirror to make sure she's buckled properly. "They are doing taste tests."

"Oh, my favorite." Violet claps her hands. "I like the cakes." I shake my head. From when she was three months old and Presley went back to work, it was with Violet strapped to her chest or being pushed in the stroller. Where she went, so did our daughter, who is now a fixture in the office. It is going to be strange when she will be in school all day, but I have no doubt she'll be running that kindergarten class with pointers for her teachers.

Even driving to the office, she is telling me when to turn. When I park next to Presley's SUV, she unbuckles herself and has the door open. She hops down and walks ahead of me, pulling open the door, and I hear her shriek, "Sofia is here!" She runs inside as I hold the door open. "I didn't know you were going to be here."

"Surprise," Sofia says, squatting down in front of her and giving her a hug. "And guess what?" She taps Violet's nose. "I'm staying all summer." Violet jumps up and down. "I'm going to need you to show me what to do." She smiles at her and stands up.

"Hi," I say, raising my hand. "How are you doing?"

"Good." She smiles and holds out her hand to hold Violet's. "It's good to be back."

"We always are happy when you are here," I tell her. Since she turned sixteen, she was coming down and visiting Harlow. She said she came down to help her with the baby, but she came to work with Clarabella one day, and well, she fell in love with the whole thing. She graduated high school two years ago and has been taking business classes. She has two more years to go, but it's safe to say she is most likely going to end up taking over the business eventually.

"How is school?" I ask, and I can see her eyes get guarded.

"Good." She looks down at Violet. "Do you want to

help me set up the plates?"

"Yes," Violet says, jumping up and down.

I look down the hallway when I hear the clicking of heels and see my wife coming toward us. I can't help but smile at her when our eyes meet. She sees Violet talking to Sofia, so she comes to me. "Hello, gorgeous." I wrap my arm around her waist and bend to kiss her. "How're you feeling?"

"Tired," she says, leaning her head on my shoulder. She is five weeks pregnant, and we just found out. We decided that it was now or never, and well, as always it took one time, and she was pregnant. "Thank God Sofia decided to take us up on the summer intern job," she says, looking over at her. "I mean, not that she needs it. She's been helping us since she turned sixteen." Presley laughs. "So much for staying on the farm and becoming a veterinarian like Harlow."

"I'm going to go and get everything set up for the meeting," Sofia says, and Presley just nods her head.

"Um, Violet?" she calls to our daughter. "Where are my hug and kiss?" She puts her hands on her hips like Violet did to me not too long ago. Violet rolls her eyes, and I have to look down and not show her I'm about to laugh. "Where is your bow?" she asks Violet.

"Daddy couldn't do it." She leans in and tries to whisper, but it doesn't come out as a whisper.

"I can do it," Sofia says. "Let's get you dressed for success." She holds out her hand for Violet, who goes over to her.

They walk out the door to the car, and Presley gets up,

standing in front of me. "God, you smell good," I say, bringing her closer to me. "Shall we go into the office?"

"Well, when you twist my arm that way," she teases as she leads me back into her office, where we go into the bathroom and have a quickie. She pulls her skirt down after she cleans up, and we walk out together.

"You guys are fucking disgusting," Shelby declares, holding Arya, her six-month-old daughter, in her arms. "There are children in the building." She holds her hands over Arya's ears. I wish I could say I was embarrassed, but with these three, nothing, and I mean nothing, could embarrass me.

"I heard you guys from my office." Clarabella waddles into the room. She's six months pregnant, but from the size of her, she's having a turkey. I'm still shocked she's having a child. "I was both disgusted and impressed."

"Okay, are we going to start this meeting?" Shelby says. "Before Sofia comes in."

"I'm so excited, Clarabella." Presley claps her hands. "She's going to be so shocked."

I look at Presley. "We are officially offering Sofia a full-time position as soon as she finishes school."

"Time to hand over the reins," Shelby says.

"Well," Presley says, "it's hers to take."

SOFIA

Two Years Later

"YOU'VE GOT THIS," Clarabella says from behind her

NATASHA MADISON

desk.

"Just remember, none of us knew what the hell we were doing," Presley tells me as she nurses her son from the couch while her other son is bouncing in the saucer right in front of her. Irish twins are what we call them. Shelby calls them a walking birth control sponsor.

"And if you need anything, we are here," Shelby reminds me, and I grab my pad.

"I've got this." I try to sound more sure of myself than I really am. "I've got this."

"Who runs the world?" Clarabella says.

"Boys and girls, according to Violet," I joke with her.

"Get out of my office and go nail that couple." She points at the door and turns and walks out.

My stomach has been in knots since last week when they handed me this client. I knew I could do it. I just have stage fright. "Here we go," I say as I pull open the door to the venue where the couple is standing with their backs to me.

I look down at my nude heels for a second, and when I look up, everything inside me stops. There standing in front of me with a blond girl holding his hand is my first love, Matthew Petrov.

Dearest Love,

Sigh, what can I say? I just can't say goodbye just yet.

Especially now that Sofia has taken over.

The stars have aligned, and it looks like not only is her first love back in her life, but she has to plan his wedding.

Will he walk down the aisle?

Who will be the bride?

You know what they say.

Only time will tell

Until September 2023

Love NM

MINE TO TAKE

Sofia Barnes

I've always loved to play dress-up.
Creating fake weddings was my childhood pastime.
Now it is my dream come true.
I've finally been handed my first client.
But nothing could prepare me for who greeted me when I walked in.
He was my first kiss, my first everything, including my first and only heartbreak.
Now I have to plan his wedding.

Matthew Petrov

My family is filled with hockey royalty.
From my grandfather to my uncle to my father.
Now it is my turn to work my way up the leaderboard.
I had everything that I've ever wanted in my life.
Or so I thought.
Nothing could prepare me for coming face-to-face with Sofia.
I knew her inside and out.
She knew my inner secrets.
Two years ago, I let her go, and now she's planning my wedding to someone else.
They say time heals old wounds. They lied.
Maybe she was just mine to take.